THE MIDNIGHT SPELL

RITE WORLD: LIGHTGROVE WITCHES
BOOK 2

JULIANA HAYGERT

COPYRIGHT

 Created with Vellum

AUTHOR'S NOTE

I hope you enjoy reading *The Midnight Test*!

Don't forget to sign up for my Newsletter to find out about new releases, cover reveals, giveaways, and more!

If you want to see exclusive teasers, help me decide on covers, read excerpts, talk about books, etc, join my reader group on Facebook: Juliana's Club!

RITE WORLD

Welcome to the RITE WORLD!

Free Novella:
The Vampire Hunt

Novellas:
The Hunter Path
The Light Calling
The Light Witch

Rite World:
The Vampire Heir (Book 1)
The Witch Queen (Book 2)
The Immortal Vow (Book 3)
The Warlock Lord (Book 4)
The Wolf Consort (Book 5)
The Crystal Rose (Book 6)
The Wolf Forsaken (Book 7)

The Fae Bound (Book 8)
The Blood Pact (Book 9)

Rite World: Blackthorn Hunters Academy
The Demons Kiss (Book 1)
The Hunter Secret (Book 2)
The Soul Bond (Book 3)
The Shadow Trials (Book 4)
The Immortal Vow (Book 5)

Rite World: Lightgrove Witches
The Midnight Test (Book 1)
The Midnight Spell (Book 2)
The Midnight Flame (Book 3)
The Midnight Secret (Book 4)

And more to come!

THE MIDNIGHT SPELL

A curious witch. A mystifying spell. And a dark destiny ...

Hazel made it into the Lightgrove Coven. Well, sort of. She made it into their initiate program. Now she needs to go through their intensive program, and only if she aces it, she'll become a full member of the famous coven.

Besides the program, she also has to attend her college classes, study for midterms, and spend some time with not-quite-her-boyfriend-yet Sean. He has been nothing but supportive, but even his patience has limits.

Hazel haphazardly tries to juggle her new life, but when she can't master her own magic, misses her class (not her fault!), lets Sean down (again, she couldn't help it!), and strange spells and marks appear among students, things spiral out of control.

On top of it all, the coven seems to be hiding something. Something dangerous.

This time, Hazel might not be able to accomplish—or save —it all.

1

"SETTLE DOWN!" A WOMAN WITH LIGHT OLIVE SKIN AND graying hair shouted.

Immediately, all the girls in the large conference room fell silent. Everyone even stopped munching on the breakfast laid out in front of them. Me included.

Last night, after the dark lightning show and the big scare, the Light Order ushered everyone to their rooms, where we were instructed to remain all night, unless a guard from the Light Order came to our doors and ordered an evacuation. Otherwise, we would be called upon in the morning.

Rodd was one of the guards leading the new girls and me to our side of the castle. I tried asking him what was happening, but besides a few glances in my direction, he didn't utter a single word, other than instructions like "follow me" and "stay in your rooms."

My mother and Amanda had been escorted to the guest wing, and as soon as they were safe in their bedrooms, they called me. We talked about what happened, but mostly, we wondered what the hell that was. Nobody knew, and I bet nobody slept well, busy worrying.

The gray-haired woman continued, "The council members are on their way, and they will explain everything."

The tension in the air increased tenfold as we waited. The girls and I exchanged a few glances, but by now, we weren't even eating anymore.

Finally, the double doors to the conference room opened, and the council members filed inside in pairs, followed by a Light Order group. This morning, Lenora, Denise, Cora, Grace, and Amelia were dressed in dress pants and button-down shirts. Even without the gowns, it was impossible not to gawk at them.

They stood at the head of the large oval table and stared down at us. Lenora's owl and Denise's red bird were perched on a nearby archway, and Grace's snake slithered on the corner.

"We know you girls have questions about last night," Denise said with a small, reassuring smile. "First, let me tell you that yes, that was unusual. And second—" She sighed as if considering her words carefully. "There isn't much we can actually disclose at the moment. The ballroom is closed, and we're conducting investigations to determine the source of the magic. Moreover—" The red-haired girl sitting beside me raised her hand. Denise turned her full attention to her. "Yes, Laini?"

"But ... do you know what that was? What the rune on the floor means?"

Denise exchanged a brief but hard look with Lenora, then turned a firm gaze to Laini. "That falls under the confidential category for now." She made a point of staring directly at each one of us, her gaze unyielding, as if challenging us to ask more questions that wouldn't be answered. Everyone stayed quiet but squirmed in their seats.

I frowned, thinking about the rune. It was one of Arianna's runes. I was sure of it, but I honestly didn't remember what they meant. These girls were mostly legacies. Shouldn't they know what it meant?

"Any more interruptions?" Lenora asked, her tone low and firm.

No one said anything.

"All right." Denise clasped her hands together. "As you all know, you're here for our initiate program, which is basically a probation period. You'll attend classes, some meetings, and events, and you'll participate in missions that will grow in difficulty with time. You have six months to prove to us that you're here because you deserve to be. Not because you're a legacy or someone who shows great power. That means that during these six months, we'll be judging your character, your traits and flaws, and how you conduct yourself." Again, she looked briefly at each one of us. "This coven is the best there is, not only in power, but because of how good-hearted we are. We are good people, good witches. We help the world, and you have to show us that's what you want too."

Denise stepped back and Lenora turned to the table. "You will be separated into three groups of five. Each group will have a mentor to whom you should report. She'll keep all your records and notes about your activities in and out of this castle, and at the end of the six months, she'll report to us. Be sure that, if we find you don't belong here, you'll be asked to leave the coven prior to the six-month period. At the end of six months, you'll have a series of tests to pass, and only then will you be a full member of this coven."

"For which we'll hold another ball," Denise added with a smile. She was trying to lighten the tense air.

The double doors opened again and three witches entered.

"These are your mentors," Lenora said. "Girls, please meet Penelope." She gestured to a tall Black woman with short, blonde-dyed hair. She wore a suit and, with her hard frame, looked much like a bodyguard. "Guinevere." Lenora pointed to a woman with white porcelain skin, faded orange hair, and an easy smile. She looked more like a best friend than a mentor. A small squirrel peeked out from a pocket in her suit jacket—her familiar. "And Moira." She gestured to a tall woman in her late thirties with hard shoulders and an even harder expression on her sharp face. Her black hair was tied back into a tight braid. She was elegant and beautiful, even with the scars streaking from her jaw to her shoulders, disappearing under the collar of her shirt. "I'll call your names. Please stand up and follow your mentor to your daily meeting room." Lenora extended her hand and a scroll appeared. She unrolled the yellow paper and read from it. "With Penelope are ..." and on she went, listing five names. The girls stood and followed Penelope out of the room as instructed. Then, she pointed to Guinevere and read five more names. Of course, I was in the last group. "And with Moira are Cleo, Belinda, Laini, Mei, and Hazel."

The remaining girls and I stood and followed Moira and her long, fast steps through a maze of corridors and down a flight of stairs, until we entered what looked like a lounge in the castle's library.

Moira closed the door as soon as I crossed the doorway.

"Sit down," she said, her tone as sharp as her expression. The other girls and I stepped farther into the lounge and sat on the uncomfortable couches in the center of the room. "My name is Moira Whitemore and I'm a legacy." With her hands behind her back, she strolled to a lone armchair between the couches. "We'll meet here every morning at seven thirty sharp. Even on weekends. No excuses, no tardiness."

She went on about the rules of the place, and I learned a few things I didn't know. Apparently, when a witch officially joined the Lightgrove coven, she could move into an apartment in the members' wing with her family. However, her family wasn't allowed into other parts of the castle. Ever. So these girls here, all legacies, had never been to this part of the castle before. Like me, they were getting a look at the place for the first time. That made me feel slightly better.

Moira took us on a tour of the castle. For about forty

minutes, we walked from grand hallways to breathtaking rooms and back to the castle entrance. From there, she led us to the council chambers, the main conference rooms, the two ballrooms, the main mess hall, the library, the initiates' rooms, the members' wing (which we didn't enter), the witches' practicing area, the Light Order wing and their training grounds, and the portals to the outside world.

To my amazement, the portal I had used to come and go from New Orleans wasn't the only one. Along the tree line, there were fourteen other portals. Thirteen of those portals had set destinations—like New Orleans, New York, Paris, Tokyo, Sydney, and other cities. However, one of those portals was a special one, only high-ranked witches could access it—its location changed according to the user's wishes.

After that, we returned to our lounge, where Moira handed us thick and empty grimoires, in which we should record everything we learn in the next six months.

"I'll take a look at those grimoires before I make my final report to the council."

That was so reassuring.

Then, she launched into a speech about the history of the Light witches. We all had heard this story a thousand times since we were little girls.

Seven hundred years ago, Arianna was a good witch in a time where bad witches were everywhere. She disbanded the Lightmist coven and founded the Lightgrove coven to protect the good witches from the trials spreading through surrounding countries, and then the world. Despite the intolerance for witches, the king learned about Arianna's good deeds and brought her to the castle to save his dear daughter, who had fallen ill because of a curse from a dark witch. After saving the little girl, Arianna gained the king's trust and joined the fight against the dark witches. That was when she began working side-by-side with Prince Thales, the heir to the crown. Eventually, Arianna and Thales fell in love but kept their romance a secret. The Brotherhood of Purity heard about Arianna's deeds and came for her. Thales sent one of his most trusted guards to protect her. However, the guard had been bought by the Brotherhood and he delivered Arianna to her death. Thales arrived in time to hold the love of his life in his arms as she died. He gathered her ashes and promised to find a way to bring her back. With the help of the sisters, Anna and Britta—the new heads of the Lightgrove coven —Thales searched for a way to bring back his love. However, Thales was killed by the Brotherhood before fulfilling his promise, and Arianna's ashes were forever lost.

Moira continued the story with Anna and Britta and their quests, among them the effort of trying to find Arianna's ashes, grimoire, and necklace—so they could try and bring her back even though that spell had been forbidden for centuries. Moira also talked a little about the other powerful coven witches—especially the Blackmarsh, Silverblood, Bluemoon, and Wildthorn covens.

"The supernatural world is changing," Moira said, a hint of wariness in her stern voice. "Blackmarsh witches don't perform sacrifices anymore; demon hunters only hunt truly evil supernaturals; the Ravensoul and Crystalflames covens remain silent and hidden; a forgotten magical werewolf pack is back, as is a coven of warlocks." I frowned. Warlocks were rare. As far as I knew, at least. For light and dark witches, the magic skipped the males, thus there were no light warlocks or dark warlocks. She waved a hand. "We'll go more in depth on all these topics during our lessons."

Next, Moira mentioned the wars between the covens, a little about the Darkmist coven history, and how close the Brotherhood of Purity had gotten to destroying us all more than once.

"Unfortunately, the Brotherhood is much stronger than we would like," she said, her voice grave. "They seem to be everywhere and they attack when we least expect it."

Seeing them at Towland had shaken me to the core, but Denise and the rest of the council assured me that had been a one-time thing, and it had been taken care of.

Then, Moira mentioned a battle with the Brotherhood a few decades back. I had never heard of this one.

"My grandmother was killed during that battle," Mei said.

"My grandfather was a member of the Light Order. He was captured and tortured," Laini said, her voice breaking. "He was rescued, but his injures were too extensive. There was nothing any witch could do for him."

I stared at them, totally lost.

Moira turned her gaze to me. "Where was your family during this battle, Hazel?"

"I ..." I closed my mouth, my throat growing dry. "I didn't even know about it until a couple of minutes ago."

Moira's eyes flamed, burning me alive. She pressed her lips tight. She snapped her head to the window, looking out at one of the internal gardens, and let out a long, shaky breath. After a minute of pure tension, she spoke again. "All right. You are all dismissed for lunch. Be back here at two."

The girls and I stood and walked toward the door. As Laini opened the door, Moira said, "Hazel?"

I glanced over my shoulder. "Yes?"

"You stay."

2

A LOUD THUD ECHOED THROUGH THE CAVERNOUS LIBRARY when Moira dropped a stack of heavy, leather bound books on a table.

"Here," she said, gesturing to the books. "These should get you started."

Anger welled up in me. I had known my mentor for only three hours, and I already hated her. Worse, she already hated me.

After finding out I didn't know the facts about one of the biggest battles between light witches and the Brotherhood, Moira asked a lot of questions about the last one hundred years in the history of witches, more specifically, of light witches. Apparently, I didn't know anything. I had believed those had been peaceful years.

"It seems your ancestors decided to hide from both light and dark witches," Moira pointed out for all the girls to hear. "The question is why?"

I argued that she was wrong. That couldn't be the case.

Maybe my mother didn't point out the book where she kept this history, and her grandmother had kept before her, the latest about the happenings in the witching world. Or, they also didn't know since my family was considered weak and unworthy. How would they know something if they had been cast aside?

But from then on, I could see, Moira was determined to pull me down.

Moira dismissed the girls and took me to the library.

"These are a few books with the latest in our history. Read them."

I gaped at her. "All right."

"You have a week to read them all."

"Wait. What?"

"I'll ask you questions about the battles in one week. You better know them all."

She turned to leave, and I exploded. "What is your problem?"

Slowly, she whirled back and glared at me. "I don't have a problem. You do."

I crossed my arms. "What is that supposed to mean?"

"I read the records of your test," she said. "I still don't know why the hell the council members let you enter the initiate program. You aren't—"

"A legacy?"

"Powerful. You're not powerful. You're almost nineteen and you don't even have an affinity." She looked me up and down. "And that too. You're not a legacy. You know *nothing* about us." She tapped her fingers on top of the book stack. "Oh, and there's one more thing I don't get.

You want to keep going to college? Why? You're a witch. Even if you don't make it after the initiate program, you can do other things, work like most witches do." She meant like ghost hunters or even Brotherhood of Purity hunters. On their own. Or I had the option to become like mother. A nothing in the witch world. No, thank you. I wanted to have options in case this witchy thing didn't work.

I was starting to believe the Lightgrove coven wasn't so pristine after all.

"That is none of your business."

"This college thing will mess with your schedule here, and even though the council authorized it, I'm telling you now. It's not going to work out."

"Like you said, the council authorized it, so I don't see what the problem is."

"Because I'm your mentor. I have to deal with you and your schedule, and worst of all, I have to make exceptions for you so you can take full advantage of the things here, which is not fair to the other girls in the program. Besides the schedule changes, don't expect any special treatment from me."

Oh, I believed I would have special treatment from her, but not in a good way. I could already see it. She would pick on me every single opportunity she had. It was going to be a nightmare.

Nevertheless, I pulled on bravado. "Well, there's nothing I can do about it. If you're worried so much about it, take it to the council yourself."

She glared at me. "Mark my words, you won't last. But

since I have to endure you *for now*, you better learn everything there is to know about the light witches. Pronto."

Without giving me time to bark a retort at her, Moira turned on her heels and walked out the library.

Bitch!

I wanted to throw the books at her, curse at her, but the librarian—an old witch with long gray hair and too many wrinkles—walked by, her gray eyes on me, as if daring me to make too much noise in her library.

With a loud sigh, I pulled the cushioned chair from under the heavy, wooden table and plopped down on it, eyes on the stack of old books. Damn it. I had to read them all? This was going to take forever.

3

———

I HAD ONLY SLEPT AT THE CASTLE FOUR OR FIVE NIGHTS IN the two weeks, but somehow that place felt more like home than my dorm. I looked around and sighed. Krissa was making a mess of everything, and apparently she thought I wouldn't come back soon, since she was using my bed as extra closet space—or a hamper. Who knew if those clothes were clean or not.

With my fingertips, I picked up her clothes and threw them on her bed, then wrote a note on a Post-it and placed it on her pillow.

Keep your shit off my bed. I still live here!

Before I flipped out and wrote more things I didn't really mean, I grabbed my books and my tote, and raced out the door. Two girls were exiting the room next door. Carrying backpacks, they both turned to me with a smile.

"Hi," one of them said.

"Hi," I said, looking from one to the other. They both had wavy, dark blond hair and brown eyes, and they definitely looked alike. "Are you new? I haven't seen you around."

"Yeah," one said. "We just moved in. I'm Brittany, and this is my sister, Andrea."

"Nice to meet you," Andrea said.

"You too." I frowned. Moving in after classes had started? What had happened to the other girls who were there last week? Odd. "Twins?"

Brittany shook her head. "No, but we certainly wish we were."

"I'm seventeen months older," Andrea said. I noticed she was about two inches shorter than Brittany, and about two inches taller than me. Andrea glanced at my tote. "Going to class?"

"You too?" I asked, and they nodded. "Same class?"

Brittany shook her head. "Oh no. I'm a sophomore and Andrea is a junior."

"Not to mention our majors are different," Andrea said.

Together, we went down the stairs while they told me more about themselves. They said the girls who lived in that room, who honestly I didn't remember their names, moved to an apartment, and since they were on the waiting list, they were offered the dorm. Andrea was an art major and Brittany was a chemistry major. Their family was originally from Europe, but they had moved from Massachusetts. They sounded chipper and friendly, and before we split to go to our separated classes, they asked for my cell phone number and promised to call.

For some reason, I liked that.

In my biology class, I sat on a desk beside the windows

facing the alleyway between two tall buildings. Several students walked by, going on with their lives.

How odd it was to look at them, living so cluelessly about the real world—about magic, witches, ghosts, evil, hunters, and much more. I often wondered how my life would have been if I hadn't known, if I hadn't been born into a witch family, with magic in my blood.

Magic that still slept inside me.

Since I had been able to access my magic on Friday the Thirteenth, I felt out of control. I felt the magic filling me up, like liquid filling a glass on the edge of spilling over. I was afraid I would accidentally use my magic at any time, without meaning to. But then, in other moments, it shut down and I couldn't even feel it.

I hoped Moira's instructions and mentorship would help control my magic and rein it in.

My gaze was still on the busy alleyway, but my mind had run from me, until I saw the cat. A black cat jumping from the side of the building to the middle of the alleyway. People yelped, tried to shoo it out of the way, complained, but the cat didn't move.

Could it ... could it be that same cat? The one that had been in Sean's and my way a couple of weeks ago?

The professor dismissed the class and I forgot about the cat. I picked up my notebook and my pen, shoved them inside my tote, and bolted toward the science building, where I knew Sean had his class.

Heart racing—not only because I had rushed across campus—I waited by the steps outside the building's door. Sean walked out. His blue eyes found mine as if they had been pulled by a magnet, and the corner of his lips tugged up. My heartbeat sped up a little more. As usual, he wore a black hoodie over a gray T-shirt that went well with his dark jeans. The hood was pulled up, hiding his dark brown hair—cut close on the sides and left longer on the top. The hood couldn't hide the few strands of hair falling over his eyes.

He halted two feet from me.

"Hi," he said, his voice deep and gruff. "I didn't think I would see you today."

"Me neither, but then …" I bit my lower lip, not sure I should be this honest. I took a deep breath and confessed, "But then I wanted to see you, so I made a point of being the first to walk out of my class."

"But don't you have another class right now?"

I nodded. "I have ten minutes before it starts."

He jerked his chin to the side. "Come on, then. I'll walk you."

We strolled from the science building to the art building and talked about random stuff. He asked me about the ceremony and my first morning at the castle as a coven member, and I asked him about his weekend.

He shrugged. "Didn't do much other than spend most of my time at the dojang."

Something tugged within me. Was he lying to me, or he was really practicing martial arts? The doubt made me feel queasy. Sean didn't have many friends. I was the closest person to him right now, and I had been away all weekend.

This witchy thing was winning me over, but I wasn't

sure how I felt about leaving Sean behind. I cared about him and I wanted our relationship to grow.

"Speaking of weekends," he started as we neared the art building. "Do you have to spend all weekend at the castle again?"

Another pang cut through my chest. Damn, I had to spend more time with him. "I'm not sure. I can check with Moira. She probably knows my entire schedule for the next six months."

Sean walked into the building with me. "Well, I was hoping to take you out on a date, so let me know when you can."

I suppressed the smile tugging at the edge of my mouth. Gosh, I wasn't this girly, this romantic, but I couldn't stop feeling the hormones dancing all over me. "I will text you as soon as I know."

"Cool," he said. We paused in front of my classroom's door. "No chance to see you tonight, right?"

"I have another class in the evening, and since I don't have class tomorrow morning, I have to spend the night at the castle."

Sean nodded, looking at the floor. "All right." He sighed, then leaned in to kiss my cheek. Oh, he wouldn't get away that easily. I turned my head and met his lips with mine. He stiffened for one quick second before his mouth claimed mine. He wound his arm around my waist and pulled me into him, tight. I let out a soft moan. Sean groaned and teased me with his tongue. I grabbed his hoodie and held on tight, fighting the noises trying to come out from my throat.

Someone coughed beside us, and we broke apart, but Sean kept his arm around me.

My professor stood at the classroom's door. "This is a school, Miss Levine, not a nightclub." Heat spread through my cheeks. "Please, come in so I can start my class."

"Yes, Mr. Jones," I said, my voice low, totally mortified.

Mr. Jones disappeared through the doorway, and I let my head fall on Sean's chest, which was rumbling with a soft laughter.

Sean kissed the top of my head. "You should go, Hazel." Nodding, I stepped back and felt the loss of the warmth from his body. He leaned in and placed a quick peck on my lips. "I'll talk to you later."

Not waiting for a response, Sean turned around and walked away. And, with my fingertips brushing my lips, I watched him until he turned a corner and disappeared from sight.

"Miss Levine," Mr. Jones called.

I jumped, startled. "Coming!"

4

I HAD BECOME A READING ZOMBIE. EVERY WAKING MOMENT, I had a book under my nose as I tried to learn as much as I could about the light witches' history. With my lessons here at the Light Castle, and my classes at Towland, I knew it would be impossible to read all the books in time for Moira's pop quiz, so I was sleeping only two or three hours each night.

Instead of being in my cozy and fluffy bed in my new fancy suite, I spent most of my nights in the cavernous library in the castle, surrounded by tall bookshelves filled with thousands of books, sconces with dimmed lights, long wooden tables and cushioned chairs, and the scent of old books. I also brought a large mug of black coffee, or I wouldn't even last to midnight. Especially after my shitty, long day. Moira continued to pick on me, arguing with me about anything and everything. The other girls were already getting used to it, and when Moira unleashed her rage on me, the girls shrank into themselves and pretended to be doing something else.

And I still wondered why I had barely talked to any of them by now.

I rolled my shoulders and shifted my weight on the chair, before leaning over the book I was reading.

Lights flickered from two bookshelves a few seconds before a witch walked out from between them. She saw me at the table, practically covered in books, and approached with a smile.

"I see someone is working hard." She halted on the other side of the table.

Now closer, I could see she wasn't much older than I was. Maybe one or two years older, and she was pretty with fair skin, freckles dotting her thin nose, and long, light brown hair. The official Lightgrove brooch was pinned to her sweater. "I understand what you're doing, but try not to overexert yourself."

I frowned. "You understand?"

She nodded. "Last semester, I was in the same situation as you." She tilted her head. "Actually, I think it was worse for me, since I had only learned about witches and Lightgrove, Lightmist, and Darkmist once I was brought here at the end of last year."

I gaped at her. Now I was intrigued. "You didn't know anything about us?"

The witch pulled out a chair and sat down across the table. She pushed a few books to the side, so we could still see each other. "No, I didn't." She extended her hand to me. "I'm Sadie Coran."

I took her hand and shook it. "I'm Hazel Levine. Nice to meet you."

"You too." Sadie pulled her hand back and sighed. "When I joined the program last January, I was new to all of this." She gestured to the books, to the library, to the castle. "I knew about my magic, but I had no idea what I was, who else was out there, or anything about the witches' history."

"And you still passed the initiate program?"

"I did, but it wasn't easy. I did exactly what you're doing. I came here every free second I had and read all the freaking books. I'm a legacy, but I might as well not be one since I had no knowledge of anything." She grabbed one of the books and flipped through some pages. "But my mentor was Guinevere, who is a lot kinder than Moira. A lot more patient too."

I brought my elbow onto the table and rested my chin on my hand. "I'm screwed."

"No, you're not." Her eyes skimmed over my body. "I can see you're determined."

"What do you mean?"

"My affinity is to see auras," Sadie explained. "Yours is a mixture of determination and fear. Most of the time, it's a good combination, since the fear will push you to be even more determined until you reach your goals."

I glanced down at the books. What was my goal? To be a light witch? To become a mere human? I still wasn't sure. I returned my gaze to Sadie. "Is it worth it? To become a full member of the Lightgrove coven."

"I've been a full member for only four months now, but

I don't regret it." She offered me a sad smile. "My life wasn't easy before I came here. I mean, it's still not easy. Fighting ghosts, demons, dark witches, the Brotherhood, and whatnot? It's not easy, but it's safer for me here. I can be who I really am. And in my opinion, it's rewarding to know I'm helping keep the world safe from evil."

I nodded, understanding her feelings. Saving the world from evil did sound noble. "Sounds like you're happy here."

Sadie nodded. "I am." Her gaze shifted to the entrance of the library, as if she was expecting something. A handful of seconds later, a Light Order member in full white armor appeared by the open doors. "I really am."

"There you are," the guy said. I had seen him before around the castle, with Rodd or talking to Denise. He approached the table and looked at me. "Hi, Hazel."

"Hm, hi." Did everyone in this damn castle know who I was?

Sadie stood. "Hazel, this is Fynn Lockwood, captain of the Light Order, Denise's son, and my boyfriend."

My eyes widened. "Oh, hi. Nice to meet you."

"Likewise," Fynn said. Then, he turned to Sadie. He looked stoic with his impressive height and armor, but what made me stare was the way he seemed attuned to Sadie. He really liked her. "Ready to go?"

She nodded before offering a small smile. "Hang in there, Hazel. I'm sure you can do it."

"Thanks," I muttered.

Hand in hand, Sadie and Fynn walked out of the library and a pang of jealousy coursed through my chest.

Sadie had Fynn here. I wished Sean was here too. I wished that if I passed this program and turned into a full member of this coven that he would be willing to become a Light Order soldier too.

I shook my head. What the hell was I thinking? Sean and I were barely dating. I couldn't expect him to abandon his life for me.

With a heavy sigh, I pushed all those thoughts away and focused on the books in front of me. I had a long night ahead of me, but I felt reinvigorated. Sadie's story had shone a light on my path.

I would find a way to succeed.

THE WEEK WAS BRUTAL.

I had barely seen Sean, save from our one class together and some walking around campus from one class to another, and Krissa had again taken over my bed in our dorm room. Andrea and Brittany had called me a few times, but I didn't answer—not because I didn't want to, but because Moira was by my side every time and wouldn't let me pick up my phone. I had studied in the library every night until I fell asleep on the books. I had seen Sadie around the castle a couple of times, but she was usually busy with the other witches or with Fynn. We had talked only once more, when we met witch Lavinia and vampire Killian who had come to seek the council's help—that had been interesting.

After reporting to Moira in the morning, I went to New Orleans for my classes. On Tuesdays and Thursdays, I had one class early in the afternoon, so I went back to the castle right away for more lessons.

"This isn't working out," Moira complained one evening. She had dismissed the other girls, but asked me to stay. "I know the council gave you permission to attend classes at Towland, but this isn't working out. You're missing important lessons."

"I can catch up. Just point out which chapters I should re—"

She scoffed. "Anyone can read chapters in the books, but can you perform the magic? Hazel, you might not be the weakest witch around anymore, but you're the one with the least control. Laini, Cleo, Belinda, and Mei have been using their full magic for quite some time now. They know how to access their power. They can control it. And because you're missing practice, you're staying behind." And staying behind meant I wouldn't become a full member when the six-month period was over. "To be honest, I don't care. If it depended on me, you would be out. But, if you want this, then show me. Show me you really want this. Show me you're as invested in becoming an important member of the Lightgrove coven as you are in graduating from whatever major you're pursuing."

Moira's speech churned in my mind the rest of the week. I tried squeezing any time I had to practice, but it still wasn't enough. Not to Moira's standards at least.

On Friday's morning check-in, Moira told me I would be working with her that evening—when I thought we all had a free night and, because of that, I had scheduled a date with Sean. I tried arguing my way out of it, but one look at her impassive face and I shut my mouth.

I texted Sean and let him know we could either cancel

our date or push it back for later. Even though he answered me through a text, I felt like his tone was upset when he told me we could go out later.

Moira took me to one of the internal gardens of the castle, the closest to the training grounds. I asked her why she didn't take me to the training grounds, and her harsh answer was witches were training there, and because I didn't have control over my magic yet, she wanted to make sure I didn't kill anyone.

The garden was large, larger than the other gardens, with stone archways, paths, and benches, and several bushes and colorful flowerbeds forming a path to the center, where a round stone fountain sprayed water into the air.

Moira stopped in front of the fountain and I halted beside her.

"I think your biggest problem is that you haven't found your affinity yet," she said, eyes on the water dripping down from the mini waterfall.

When a witch first got her powers, she also got an affinity, or a gift as some called it. All witches could perform all kinds of magic, depending on their powers, but light witches also had a special gift, something they could do better than everything else, better than the other witches. Some had affinity for elemental magic, some had affinity for potion making, others could teleport or read someone else's mind. As for me, since I had blocked my magic, my affinity had escaped me. Maybe I was never supposed to have one.

I sighed, agreeing with her. "That makes sense. So, your plan is to test all possibilities to see what sticks."

"Yes." She turned to look at me. "Get ready, it's going to be a long night."

I started to protest, saying I had things to do, but again the look on her face and the tone of her voice told me it wasn't up for discussion. My only hope would be to find my affinity quickly so I could leave soon.

We started with water from the fountain, then air, then earth, then fire from a lighter Moira had brought with her, then the fifth element, spirit, but none of them called to me. Not that I couldn't do magic with them. When I relaxed enough from Moira's intense scrutiny, I was able to let my magic go and actually do some cool things, but not enough to believe I had found my affinity.

Two hours had passed when we moved on to other kinds of magic, and I was itching to reach for my cell phone and call Sean. He was probably already pissed at me, and all I could do was apologize.

After we were done with the elements, Moira pulled out a long list and my heart sank. If we followed the list and didn't find my affinity until the end, I wouldn't be leaving this garden until Sunday night.

I sat down on a bench, feeling frustrated and quite tired.

Moira folded her arms and glared down at me. "What are you doing?"

"Resting for a few seconds," I said, trying my best not to sound intimidated by her.

"I didn't say it was time for a break," she snapped. "Get up and let's keep this on."

"Just give me a moment, okay? I used plenty of magic and need a break."

"Do you think I want to be here with you? I have more important things to do, you know, than waste my time training a non-legacy girl who thinks she's better than anyone because she passed a stupid test." The venom in her voice made me stiffen. Was that what everyone thought of me, or was it just this hardass witch? "Let me tell you something. I don't know what the hell the council saw in you, why they let you in the coven, but you aren't better than the others. In fact, you're the worst witch I have seen in a long, long time."

I gasped. "What the ...? You barely know me. I have no idea what I did to deserve this treatment but—"

"But I'm still your superior, your mentor, and you will shut up when I tell you to. So shut up."

I stood. "You can't tell me to shut up."

"Yes, I can," she said, her voice rising, along with the hate in her eyes. "I'm the one writing your reports, remember? Unless you want me to tell the council how you mess up every magic you do, you'll shut up."

"You wouldn't," I whispered, totally shocked. She ... was she this evil? She hated my guts so much that she would lie on her reports about me to get rid of me. Fear and frustration snaked their way into my spine. What if I found an affinity and mastered my magic the way I was supposed to, or even better, and still she messed me up?

There was nothing I could do about that now, other

than do my best to impress her and pray she was truthful on her reports. At least, until I thought of another solution.

"Test me and you'll find out." Moira let out a long breath, as if expelling the hate from her lungs, and looked at the list. "Now, let's continue."

She went on telling me the next item on the list—temporary invisibility—and explaining how to do it. Besides all my efforts, this was one of the gifts that you could do it, or you couldn't. And to my dismay, I couldn't.

After another string of curses, Moira went on with the list and we practiced for another three hours.

6

It was almost midnight when I finally got through the portal to the French Quarter, which was still in full swing, and got a cab to Sean's building. I paid extra for the driver to go a little faster.

Once there, I climbed up the steps and halted a few paces from the front door.

The black cat stood there, right at my feet, blocking my way to the door.

I gawked at it, wondering why this cat—it was the same cat, wasn't it?—kept showing up wherever I was.

"Shoo, kitty," I said, pushing it aside with the tip of my boot. The cat meowed and circled my legs. "What do you want? Food? Sorry, I have nothing on me other than gum."

He meowed again, but I ignored him as I rang the intercom to Sean's apartment. A full minute passed and there was no answer. I backtracked a few steps and looked up to both windows I knew belonged to his apartment.

They were closed and there was no light coming from them.

I sighed and was surprised when I felt tears burning the back of my eyes. Shit. This was all my fault. I had promised him a date and now was too late—he was either sleeping, or out by himself.

I gasped—what if he wasn't out by *himself*?

No, no. Sean wouldn't do that to me, would he?

A heavy wave of emotions washed over me, and I sat on the steps, feeling completely exhausted—emotionally and physically.

Moira and I had practiced for five hours, going through two-thirds of the list, and I hadn't found any affinity. I was starting to believe I was a lost cause. Maybe she was right and I didn't belong in the Lightgrove coven.

The cat came back and sat at my feet again.

"What do you want?" I snapped. "Why have you been following me?"

The cat stared at me, as if he could tell me his exact reasons through his black eyes.

"Damn cat," I muttered, pushing off the steps.

I walked to my dorm building, aware that the cat was still following me. But when I stopped to unlock my building's door and looked back, the cat had disappeared.

Too exhausted to care, I shrugged it off and walked into my building. I was about to unlock my dorm's door when Andrea walked out of her room.

"Hi!" she said, with a big smile on her face.

"Hey," I said.

She lost the smile. "Are you okay?"

I shrugged. "Had a rough day."

"Oh." She looked over her shoulder to her bedroom. "Hm, Brittany and I are watching horror movies and eating ice cream and cookies and brownies with hot fudge and toppings. I'm going to buy more soda from the vending machine down the hall." She showed me the cash in her hand. "But we're about to start watching *The Shining*. You're welcome to join us."

"Hm ..." Why not? They seemed cool enough, and right now, I could use a friend—though, preferably I would have made a friend among my little witchy group, but everyone there looked at me as if I was an alien that needed to be dealt with. I assumed I wouldn't be making any friends there. Not for now. "I do have a weakness for horror movies."

She beamed again. "Cool! Come in." She stuck her head inside the room. "Hey, Brit, Hazel is joining us."

I walked in and found Brit leaning over a small coffee table piled high with all the treats they were having tonight. I sighed. It was as if they were expecting me with my favorite kind of movie and comfort food.

"Hey, girl," Brittany said. "Come in!"

"I'll be right back," Andrea said, heading out to grab more soda.

"Here." Brittany handed me a clean ice cream bowl and spoon. "Dig in."

"Thanks."

And just like that, I felt a little better about my day—

about my failure with Moira and Sean. I couldn't erase those, no, but I could at least try to forget them for now, with the promise that I would do better the next day.

7

EVEN THOUGH I WENT TO BED LATE, I WAS UP EARLY THE next morning.

I took a long, hot shower, got dressed in leggings, a thin sweater, and knee-high boots, and then stopped by the main campus coffee shop and grabbed breakfast for me and Sean. I was shaking as I walked up the steps in front of his building and rang the intercom.

After a minute without answer, my heart started failing. What if he was still sleeping because he was out late with the gods knew who? Or he was at the window, looking down at me and purposely ignoring me.

I sighed, and pulling courage from deep within me, I rang the intercom again.

Another minute passed and nothing.

Sighing, I turned to walk away and almost bumped into him.

"Oh, hi," I said, stepping back.

"Hey," Sean said, his tone a little down. He wore his

martial arts pants and a sleeveless black tank, with the top and his black belt over his shoulder. His toned arms gleamed with a sheen of sweat. His hair and shirt were damp, but he had a cigarette in his hand. His face though, the closed way he looked at me, with his jaw tense and his eyebrows turned down, it made my heart hurt.

"Sean, I'm so sorry about last night," I blurted out. "My mentor is the worst. She hates my guts and she is trying to turn my life into a living hell. I wanted to text you, to let you know she was working the soul out of me, but I couldn't get to my phone, not without calling up her wrath. And—"

"Hazel." His tone was harsh, and I clamped my mouth shut. I wanted to avert my eyes and run away, but I forced myself to look at him, even when the hardness of his stare brought tears to the backs of my eyes. I swallowed them, determined not to cry in front of him. Then, to my surprise, he sighed and his shoulders relaxed. "It's ... it's okay."

"W-what?"

"I understand, I think." He paused to take a drag of his cigarette. He let the smoke out slowly, then sighed again. "I understand that this witch thing is different and follows a different set of rules and expectations and schedules, and that I'll never completely get it, or be able to be a part of it, but ..."

"But what?"

"I miss you," he whispered. "After ... after that night, I thought we had connected and that we were trying to become a real couple, you know."

My heart fluttered. "I know. I mean ..." I cleared my throat. "Me too. That's what I want."

"It has been almost a month, and we haven't even been on a date. We barely see each other outside of class."

I didn't know what to say other than, "I'm sorry, Sean. I'm doing the best I can ..." And I was failing miserably.

He took a last drag of his cigarette, threw it away, then he took a step closer to me. "How about we try again?" He brushed aside my hair, letting his fingertips run along my jaw and neck. I leaned into his touch. "After all, I like you."

"And I like you," I whispered.

Sean wrapped his arms around my waist and brushed his lips against mine. "It's a deal, then." And then he kissed me, really kissed me. His tongue teased mine and my knees weakened. I would have crumbled to the ground if it weren't for his strong arms holding me up. I used magic to set our breakfast bag on the ground and then wrapped my arms around his neck, pulling him closer to me. The cigarette taste on his tongue was erased by the fierce way his lips moved against mine.

Sean backed me to the wall beside the door, pressing his hard body against mine and drew a moan out of my mouth. He groaned and pressed even tighter, molding my body to his. My head spun and I melted into him.

The building's front door flew open, and startled, we jumped apart. A lady walked out with two little kids, giving us wary looks, and Sean and I turned our backs to her so she wouldn't see us laughing. We remained like that until she was out of sight.

Still smiling, Sean picked up the bag from the ground. "I believe you brought me breakfast."

"Yup," I said, returning his smile. "I wanted to make sure my apology would be heard."

He leaned in for a quick peck. "It was heard. And now I want breakfast." He caught my hand in his. "Come on."

With my hand in his, Sean led me to his apartment. Once he closed the door behind us, Sean was on top of me again. He took the coffee shop bag from me, settled it on the floor, and pushed me against the door. His hands on my waist and his mouth on mine. I melted into him, desperate to touch him, to feel him, to taste him. Sean slid his hands down around my ass, to my thighs, and tugged on them. I wrapped my arms around his neck, and he pulled me up, my legs around his waist. Without breaking the kiss, he carried me to the couch, where he laid me down and climbed over me.

I sighed in delight at his weight pressing against me, the feel of his hips rubbing against mine, the taste of his mouth, the feel of his ripped arms on my hands.

I tugged on his top and he let me pull it, breaking the kiss only so I could take it off completely. I threw it to the side and he leaned into me again, his lips brushing against mine. Loving to explore him, I ran my hands up his arms, around his shoulders, and down his chest and stomach.

And Sean groaned, breaking the kiss.

I stilled. "What is it?"

"It's nothing," he muttered through gritted teeth. He came for me again, but I could see he wasn't okay. I pushed on his shoulders and stared at him. There, at his side, was a purpling bruise almost as large as my hand.

"What the hell? That's not nothing." I sat up, forcing Sean to scoot from over me. He sat beside me, our legs touching. "What happened?"

Sean ran a hand over his hair. "I was frustrated last night and went to the dojang to train. One of the instructors-in-training was there, and we sparred for hours. And well, we sparred for real." He turned his hands, showing me his red knuckles, and then he turned his back to me, where another smaller bruise was settling. "Don't worry," he said, his voice a little lighter. "My opponent didn't fare much better."

I stared at him, torn between shock and horror. So, this was all because of me. He had been frustrated I hadn't come for our date and he decided to kick someone's ass instead.

That was kind of messed up.

I swallowed hard, not sure what to say.

I wasn't mad at him; I was mad at myself for not being there for him. Sean had suffered a lot already, and here I was, making his life worse.

"I'm sorry," I whispered.

Sean took my hands in his. "For?"

"For not being here."

"You already apologized for that, and I already accepted your apology. It's okay."

But it wasn't. Once more, here I was, pretending I could do it all, be it all, have it all. To go to college like a normal person, to train to be a real light witch, to have a human boyfriend.

I didn't want to think about it, but I knew that at some point, something would have to give.

Pushing those thoughts away, I stood and picked up the bag from the floor. "I think our breakfast is cold now." I set the bag on the coffee table in front of the couch and sat beside Sean again.

"I can fix that." With a small smile, Sean took the bag to his kitchen. He put the coffee into mugs and heated them up in the microwave. He did the same with my muffin and his ham and cheese croissant. He came back with the mugs and plates. "Almost like new." I nodded, still lost in thought, but trying to pull through. Sean nudged his knee on mine. "Hey. Just forget about whatever is bothering you. Think about us, about now."

I stared at him, my eyes locked on his blue ones. He was right. I couldn't change what happened yesterday. I could only try to do better.

"Come here," I said, picking up two pillows from the couch and placing them on the floor between my legs. "Sit."

With a cocked eyebrow, Sean obeyed. He sat between my legs, his back to me, and I started massaging his back, shoulders, and neck.

He let out a contented sigh. "I could get used to this."

I had to say, this was for my benefit too, since I could touch his lean body and rigid muscles without looking like a creep. I massaged him while we ate and talked about random things—school, grades, his martial arts training and how it was helping with his depression, even though he had to train harder to catch up to the level he was before quitting, how he was talking to his parents a little more now, and how Moira wanted me to quit the initiate program.

Being like this with Sean, talking and touching and eating together, felt normal, felt good.

Yeah, I guess I could get used to this too.

8

UNFORTUNATELY, I COULDN'T STAY LONG WITH SEAN because I had to go to the French Quarter and meet with the other witches and our mentors. We gathered at the corner of Bourbon and Dumaine, and I was surprised to see members of the Light Order patrolling the area. They wore their gray uniforms, with some captains in white, but I could bet they had their clothing enchanted so the humans wouldn't notice something amiss. People dressed weirdly in New Orleans, but a group of fierce looking men in billowing white cloaks? That wouldn't go unnoticed.

All fifteen girls were together in the middle of the street, the girls of my own group—Laini, Cleo, Belinda and Mei—stood the closest to me. And Moira, looking as stoic and unfriendly as ever, stood beside us.

"All right," Moira said, turning to our group. "The humans here think we're a tourist group, all wearing the same ridiculous shirt, so don't worry about what they see or don't see." She looked around us. "Your assignment is to walk around the streets of the French Quarter and identify the supernatural beings you encounter. Do not engage them. We're not here on a mission; we're to learn, and that means to identify them and report back to me."

I frowned, remembering when I started sensing and seeing the supernaturals around here a couple of weeks ago. It had happened rarely since then, but it made me wonder if it really had been because of the weak spell Khalisa had put on that fake bone pendant, or if it had been me.

"What if they engage us?" Cleo asked.

"The supernaturals here shouldn't try to engage you because they fear the Light Order," Moira said. "But, in case they prove to be stupid, the Light Order will intervene and keep you safe." She looked at each one of us, and I could swear her already hard expression grew harsher when her eyes met mine. "Any more questions?" We all shook our heads. "All right. Keep close to each other and at least to one member of the Light Order. Now, go." She waved us off.

The girls and I turned around and walked down Bourbon Street. At first, it was hard to see anything along the crowded street. I couldn't fail this assignment. Otherwise Moira would have another reason to skin me alive in front of everyone. I inhaled deeply and called my magic. I opened it up, ordering my senses to become stronger, faster, more sensitive.

"I can't see anything," Laini said, her tone filled with disgust. "Honestly, I don't want to see anything. Other supernaturals are quite disgusting."

One corner of my lips curled up. "I know where we can see them," I said, taking the lead. Of course, Laini hesitated, but the others didn't. They all followed me until we were across the street from The Dark Veil.

The last time I had been here, I had shaken so hard, but this time, I womanned up because I wanted to show off to Laini, who could be a big bitch, and because I knew the Light Order was close by.

"Holy cow," Belinda said, holding on to Cleo's arm. "I'm not the only one seeing this, right? There's a bunch of supes in that shop."

I nodded, taking stock of the werewolf sitting by the large window, the two witches right behind him, and the demon entering the shop. I knew there were classes of demons—lesser, neutral, higher, and grand—but I couldn't tell them apart.

When a succubus left the shop and stared at us, a little sliver of fear snaked down my spine.

"Oh, damn, we're caught," Mei muttered.

But the succubus's eyes shifted a few yards to our side. I followed her gaze and found Rodd and Fynn standing at the corner of the street, their attention on us and the shop. The succubus huffed and moved along, as if we were all normal humans.

After that, we continued our walk around the French Quarter and occasionally saw other supernaturals here and there. We saw two witches, but we couldn't tell if they were light or dark witches, or another kind altogether.

After an hour walking aimlessly, and already annoyed about Laini complaining—about the weather, the people, the weak witches—I slowed my steps until I was right in front of Rodd and Fynn, who had been following my group since the beginning of this assignment.

"So, when will we be done?" I asked them, without actually looking at them.

"Just a little longer," Fynn told me.

"We will gather everyone where we started in less than thirty minutes," Rodd added. I nodded. "Why? Aren't you having fun?"

I scoffed. "Hanging with Laini for this long? If I hear one more of her comments, I'll be sick." I sighed. "The worst part is that I can feel the others don't really agree with her, but they won't stand up to her either."

"It's because she's a legacy," Fynn said. "I mean, all of them are, but Laini's mother is a high-ranked light witch."

I frowned and glanced at the guys. "High ranked?"

Rodd nodded. "If something were to happen to one of the council members, her mother would take the open spot."

Oh, good to know.

"Sadie went through the same," Fynn added, surprising me. "She was a legacy, but she had no knowledge about us and our history. Thankfully, Guinevere is a patient mentor, but there were other girls in her group who were just as"—he paused, pressing his lips together—"spoiled as Laini."

"But she made it," I reminded him.

A small smile adorned his lips. "She did."

I smiled too. It was so cute to see how into her he was.

Sadie had been nice to me; I was glad she had someone like Fynn in her corner.

"You'll make it too," Rodd said.

I snorted. "Not if Moira has a say in it."

"Don't let her intimidate you," he said. "She's more bark than bite."

"I seriously doubt that," I muttered. I wasn't afraid of Moira per se, but I was afraid of her power over my future. If she wanted, she could act on her threats and have me expelled from the Light Castle in five minutes flat.

"You know ..." Rodd looked down at his feet before returning his eyes to me. "Moira is my mother."

I tripped on my own feet. "What?"

Rodd reached for me, but I straightened before I could faceplant. "Yeah. Sorry, I didn't tell you before."

I inhaled deeply and shook my head. He didn't owe me anything.

Did his mother know he danced with me during the welcoming ceremony? Maybe that was why she didn't like me and was giving me a hard time. My mind reeled with the new information I had gathered. Even though I had no feelings toward him, I probably should stay away from Rodd so Moira wouldn't add another item to her why-I-hate-Hazel list.

We fell silent as we continued our stroll through the French Quarter. At some point, the girls stopped by the Cafe Du Monde to buy beignets and coffee, and I gladly joined them for those ten minutes, because who could say no to beignets?

But a few moments later, it was time to go. At the

appointed time, we met at the starting point again. My group was the first to arrive, and we waited for the other ten girls with the three mentors and some Light Order soldiers.

"What is taking the others so long?" Guinevere asked, looking around.

"I don't know," Penelope said. "Maybe I should go and—"

She stopped abruptly as thunder echoed through the air.

Everyone gasped and jumped back when a flash of dark lightning struck from the sky right in the middle of our group, as loud and bright and powerful as it had happened during the welcoming ceremony two weeks ago.

The humans around us didn't see the crackling flames burning the stones on the ground, but some of them looked up and commented, "It looks like it's going to rain."

"How ..." How didn't they see it?

Moira and the other two mentors exchanged more than looks, then nodded their chins, and stepped between their groups and the spreading dark flames.

"Look." Mei pointed to the ground.

Smoke curled in the air from the flames, but we could see it was doing something. The same thing it had done before. It took longer this time for the flames and their sizzling sound to fade away, but when it did, we all gaped at the rune engraved on the ground. I noticed it was similar to the one from the ballroom, but it was slightly different.

"What does that mean?" Laini asked.

Several other girls voiced similar questions.

Without a word, Guinevere and Penelope ran off with a handful of Light Order soldiers at their feet, probably to fetch the other ten girls.

Moira conjured a little stool out of thin air and stepped on it. "Quiet!" As if a whip had been sliced through the air above our heads, we all shut up in less than one second. "This ... this isn't our concern. However, we need to go back to the castle at once. The Light Order will escort you all."

She jumped off the stool and it disappeared. And then, like a sheep flock, we were escorted to the antique store where we used the portal to go back to the Light Castle.

9

ONCE BACK AT THE LIGHT CASTLE, THE MENTORS AND THE council didn't offer any explanation about what had happened in the middle of the French Quarter. They simply told us to keep on with our activities as normal.

Yeah, right.

My afternoon was spent with my group and Moira, talking about the supernatural beings we had encountered this morning, and if engaged, how to deal with them. We even practiced what to do in enchanted practice dummies.

The fifteen of us had dinner together in the great hall, then were bidden good night and sent to our bedrooms.

Nobody had said anything about staying in our bedrooms, so once it was late enough, I slipped out and made my way to the library on the first floor. I had been doing that almost every night for the last several days, though then it had been to study. Now, it would be for research.

The place was dark and empty. It felt like I was

entering a mysterious cavern. Using my magic, I lit the candles in the sconces around the main part of the library.

I set the candle I had brought with me to hover over my shoulder, so I could browse through the books with my hands free, and started walking around the library's shelves. After about thirty minutes, my hope of finding something dwindled. There were books about anything and everything in here. There had to be books about runes, but where? In which section?

I used magic to help me.

Closing my eyes, I thought of both runes I had seen after the dark flame shows. I channeled my magic and asked it to take me to those runes. A couple of minutes passed and nothing happened, but I didn't want to give up so easily. I called more of my magic, and its unstable power filled my veins. Once more, I focused on the runes and asked to be taken to them.

A faint tug pulled at the center of my chest. With a gasp, I followed it, going deeper into the library and the dark shelves. I halted in front of a long shelf lined with books about symbols. I skimmed the spines and pulled out the ones that looked promising. I sat down on the hard floor with the books scattered around me, and flipped through them.

I found complicated languages, hidden symbols, hiero-glyphs, several books on different runes. I had also found several books about Arianna's runes, and it was then that I realized something: both runes I had seen looked like Arianna's runes, but they had minor differences. Tiny lines that turned and twisted in different ways. If I hadn't been here, holding these books in my hands and paying attention to it, I would have never noticed.

However, now that I knew they were different, I couldn't find the two runes anywhere. First, because I didn't know what they were called or how to look them up. Second, because even though I flipped through the books, searching for the symbols, there was no mention of the runes anywhere.

Damn it.

What could those runes mean? Why were the council and the other witches keeping it a secret from the rest of us? Did they even know what they meant, or were they as clueless as I was? What were they doing to find out? Where would they find out? There had to be a place where they could find out about these runes. But where?

The sound of footsteps inside the library made me jump, my heart racing. I dimmed the light from the candle and shoved the books back into their places, hoping they were in the right spot, and scurried away from that shelf. I didn't want to be seen researching the runes.

The footsteps grew closer, and I was sure I was going to be caught. I grabbed the candle in my hand, stopped in front of another shelf, and picked up the book closest to me.

"Hazel?"

I gasped, pretending to have been startled, and turned to the person approaching me. Then, I saw who it was and frowned. "Rodd. Hi."

"What are you doing here?"

"I—I was studying."

He halted beside me and glanced at the cover of the book in my hand. "The Essential Difference Between Higher and Grand Demons? That's what you like to read?"

Shit. "Oh, yeah, you know. It's a great read to make you sleep." My cheeks flamed with embarrassment, and I prayed he didn't notice my lie.

He lifted a brow at me. "If you say so." He glanced around. "I know you've been studying a lot at night, but you shouldn't be out this late."

"Why not? I thought the castle was safe."

"It is, but we prefer knowing where each witch is, just in case something happens."

I nodded. "I understand." Clutching the book to my chest, I followed Rodd as he walked toward the library's main doors. I bit my lip to stop the words from coming out, but that wasn't enough. "So you're Moira's son."

"Yup." He glanced at me. "I know she can be intense sometimes b—"

"Sometimes?"

One corner of his lips tugged up. "All right. All the time. I know, believe me."

There were so many questions I wanted to ask him, but I was afraid of how he would interpret them. What if he went babbling to his mother about my questions? Worse, what if he told his mother I had been in the library, close to the symbols and runes section, at this time of the night.

I gasped. "Rodd, you won't te—"

"Don't worry. I won't tell my mother that you were here if"—he stopped at the library's doors—"you promise to not wander around the castle alone at night."

"I promise."

"Also, hm." He ran a hand through his hair. "If you agree to go on a date with me."

I froze. "Hm, Rodd, I'm sorry but ... I'm seeing someone."

"Oh." He looked away from me, and I could see his jaw ticking. After a heartbeat, he returned his eyes to me, a small smile plastered on his lips. "I'm sorry I asked. I wouldn't have if I had known."

"It's okay. But ... will you tell your mother?"

He shook his head. "No. Don't worry about it. If she asks, I'll say you were studying." He jerked his chin toward the hallway behind me. "Come on. I'll walk you back to your bedroom where you can read The Essential Difference Between Higher and Grand Demons, and fall sleep."

Smiling, I nodded and let him escort me to my bedroom.

"Thanks," I said, once we reached my door.

Rodd pursed his lips for a moment, then said, "I hope your boyfriend is treating you well, Hazel, because you don't deserve anything less." He bowed his head at me. "Good night."

"Good night," I whispered as he walked away.

10

I ALMOST MISSED MY FIRST CLASS MONDAY MORNING because of the damn check-in with Moira. She went on and on, reviewing what we did on the weekend and explaining to us in detail what we would do this coming week. Something told me she was doing it on purpose, just to frustrate me and make me late. She wanted to see me fail.

But I didn't give her that satisfaction. She let us out with not a minute to spare. But she tried to stop me.

"You shouldn't leave the castle," she said in a dark tone, darker than usual.

"Why?" I asked. If she said because she didn't like me trying to be both a witch and a human, I would scream.

Surprisingly, she looked into my eyes and said, "Because there are things happening. It might be dangerous."

I confess that made me waver. If she, who absolutely

didn't like me, was worried about whatever was happening —it could only be the dark flames and the runes, right— then shouldn't I be too?

No, I wouldn't cave. If I did, then I would miss everything else.

I left the Light Castle without wasting any time. I would have to rush to campus and get to my classroom, if the traffic and everything else was perfect. It wasn't, but I ran when I could and I told the Uber driver I would tip him double if he drove fast.

I entered my classroom and sat at my desk with four minutes to spare.

I sighed in relief. Until Sean didn't show up for the class—it was the only one we shared—and the professor came in and started his boring lecture. Which got me thinking ... maybe Moira was right about this. Not that I wanted to give her credit for anything, but maybe she was onto something. This witchy thing ... it was nice. Even with the hard time she was giving me, I liked being a witch. If the council approved me as a full member at the end of the six month period, I would be content. I wanted this witchy thing now. Most of the witches there didn't go to college. They had their own education, about all kinds of subjects, but especially about magic. And that was all they needed to follow this profession.

Did I want that for me? Did I want to live in that castle for the rest of my life? Did I want to get married and raise a family there? One of the castle's wings belonged to the families of the witches within the coven—and the ones that hadn't officially joined the coven or the Light Order and couldn't roam the rest of the palace. That could be an option, but ... what about Sean? I mean, he was the guy in my life now, and I could see myself falling hard for him and dreaming of a future with him, having a future with him. What would he think about living in the castle? About raising our kids there? I gasped. Holy crap, what the hell was I doing? Dreaming of having kids with Sean? We had barely started dating. I couldn't even call him my boyfriend yet. This was crazy.

I shook my head, trying to push away those thoughts, but they moved to the back of my mind while the part about college and the witchy job came back in full force. What did I want? Not thinking about Sean or my mother's dream or Amanda's enthusiasm. What did I want?

I wasn't sure. Not yet.

I guess the first step would be to wait and see if I was accepted into the Lightgrove coven for good. Then, I would consider my choices. Then, I would make a choice.

However, the way things were going, I wasn't so sure I would have a choice. Sunday morning, Moira had dragged me out of bed at six to continue what we started Friday night. She took me to that same garden, and during the next five hours, we went through the rest of her list and even repeated a few items that had looked promising. But nothing was my affinity. Nothing. Moira wondered if there was something else she was missing, because every witch had an affinity, even a small one. That meant I wasn't truly a witch—her words, not mine.

I sighed again, feeling like total crap.

The moment the class ended I texted Sean.

Me: *Are you okay?*

Sean: *Right, sorry. I stayed up late at the dojang last night and slept in. I'll see you later.*

It made sense, but at the same time, it felt like a lie. No, no, there was no reason for Sean to lie to me.

Right?

My second class ended, and I walked out of the building, my head back on the dilemma of me posing as a witch.

"What's the matter?" Sean asked.

I halted, with a shriek lodged in my throat. "Holy ... you almost gave me a heart attack." I rested my hand over my racing heart.

One corner of his lips tugged up. "Sorry." He caught my hand and pulled me out of the way of the students who were coming up and down the stairs, entering and exiting the building. "Hi," he whispered, leaning into me. He brushed his lips on mine, and I swayed into him. With a chuckle, he pulled back.

"Come back here," I said, tugging his hoodie.

"Answer me, first." He ran a fingertip over my forehead, smoothing the worry lines. "I can see something isn't right." Instead of speaking, I stepped into him, wound my arms around his waist, and buried my face in his chest. His arms were around me in an instant. "Hey, you're worrying me."

I sighed and turned my face, resting my cheek on his chest. "It's nothing really ..."

I had already complained about Moira to him before; I

didn't want to waste the precious minutes I had with him by repeating myself.

"It's that mentor again, isn't it?"

I groaned. "She hates me."

"No, she doesn't."

I pulled back and looked up at him. "Yes, she does. I know she wants to screw me over. I bet she's plotting something so I will mess up big and be dismissed early."

"Hazel," he said, running a hand through my hair. "Even if that's true, I know you won't let her screw you over like that. I know you can overcome whatever shit she throws at you. You're that strong."

"You give me too much credit."

"That's because you're too badass."

I rolled my eyes. "You saw me in action once, and that was the most extreme thing I had to do. Ever."

"And because I saw that, I know you can be just as badass again. Or even more badass."

I just shook my head. "Okay, all right. Can we change subjects? What are you doing here?"

He grinned and it was too beautiful. My heart skipped. "I knew you would be free for lunch, so I talked to my professor, told him I was sick, and he's going to let me attend the other section of the class later today."

I gasped. "So you can have lunch with me."

"Yup."

I wanted to throw myself at him, wrap my arms tight around his neck, and kiss him like I had never kissed him before, but there were too many students coming and going, and I wasn't one for public displays.

So, I just smiled. "That's great."

He offered me his hand. "Where do you want to have lunch?"

I took his hand. "As long as you're with me, I don't really care."

11

GOOD THINGS DIDN'T LAST LONG.

After a nice lunch at a cozy diner, Sean and I spent another hour together, walking around campus and talking about anything and everything. I had told him about the assignment the other witches and I had on Saturday morning, and the fire that struck out of nowhere, and that had been the reason we couldn't leave the castle the entire weekend. But I didn't tell him they didn't want me to come back to class—not only because it was messing up my schedule around the castle, but because they didn't know what the rune meant and they preferred their witches remain at the castle.

In turn, Sean told me almost nothing about himself. I mean, he said he wasn't doing much other than going to classes, running at least three times a week, and going to the dojang every evening, but that was it. He didn't tell me what he did during the rest of the weekend, or what he did in his free time. And I didn't ask. Sean was still reserved and serious, and I was afraid that if I pushed him, he would snap and break up with me. I had to give him some time to grow used to me.

Then, our hour together was up. Sean still had two more classes that afternoon, but I didn't. Since he was busy, I found myself trying to figure out what to do. I could return to the castle and work with Moira and the other girls, but I really wasn't in the mood.

I needed some alone time. Some me time. And I knew how to spend that time.

It had been a little over a month since I last entered the Midnight Cauldron—the day after Friday the Thirteenth —but it was still the same. Dark shelves filled with knick-knacks a tourist would like.

"Evening, my child," the witch doctor said, grinning at me.

I nodded in acknowledgment. "How are you, Khalisa?"

She clicked her tongue. "Can't complain." She appraised me with her large, dark eyes. "I don't think witches from the Lightgrove coven need my supplies. So, what brings you back to my little place?"

I halted across the counter from her, being careful with my tone, so no wandering customer could hear me. "First, I'm not a full member yet. Second, it's not like they need to know." I winked and her face softened. "Remember the newspaper clippings you showed me?" She gave me a curt nod. "Well, I was wondering, can I look at them again?"

She tilted her head, her dreadlocks swishing with the movement. "Why?"

"I ... That story you showed to me, about Sean and

Lizzie and Doug. Well, I was able to free Lizzie, but before leaving, she told me Doug is still around, though she doesn't know where. I've searched the city, areas I thought might be haunted by ghosts. I also visited his old house, his dorm, and the places he used to go to the most, but I can't find him. I wanted to read that article again to see if they mention something about him that can help me locate his ghost."

The witch doctor watched me for a minute, then beckoned for me to walk around the counter and follow her to another room. Judging by the small, round table in the middle, the three wooden chairs around it, the tarot cards and bones and other unrecognizable things on the table, this was where she told people's fortunes.

For a moment, I wondered if she really could. If her fortune-telling was real or not. And if it was, did she tell everyone the truth, or did she tell them what she thought they wanted to hear? I bit my lower lip, wondering, wanting to ask her to read mine. I wanted to know what it would say about the coven and about Sean. But, if she really could tell the future and told me about it, what would I make of it? What if I didn't like what I heard? Would I try to change it? Perhaps it was better if I didn't know.

Khalisa pushed the cards and bones aside and dropped the heavy binder with the clippings on the table.

"Here it is," she said, pulling out a chair for me.

"Thanks." I sat down and opened the binder, checking the dates to find the article I was looking for.

Khalisa took another seat. "I don't think you'll find anything in that article."

I frowned. "Why not?"

She shrugged before taking the binder from me. I was about to argue, but she started flipping through the pages, looking for something. "Here," she said, turning the binder back to me but keeping a finger tucked between the pages. "This might help you."

Young Man Dies on Halloween Night

I gasped, shifting my gaze to the corner of the article, where the date was. One year before Lizzie and Doug.

"Holy shit," I muttered.

I skimmed the article. This guy, Karl, had died at the Hotel Monteleone, the night of Halloween. He was there with a friend on a dare to find ghosts, and his friend was committed for saying there were ghosts at the hotel and that Karl was one of them—he was violent about it.

Then, Khalisa turned the pages to where her finger was. "And here."

Boyfriend and Girlfriend Found Dead on Friday the Thirteenth.

This article was dated almost two years prior to Lizzie and Doug. Peter and Anna had gone into Saenger Theater on a Friday the Thirteenth; nobody knew why. Their parents thought they were having fun, trying to scare each other. In the end, Anna died at the theater while Peter was able to call for help, saying there were ghosts attacking them, before also dying. Months later, Peter's parents were interviewed by a fake ghost hunter who was famous on

YouTube. His mother told the ghost hunter that she sometimes saw Peter's ghost around, and he always begged for help, but she didn't know what to do and ended up crying until he disappeared.

I looked at the witch doctor. "Are you trying to tell me all these are connected?"

She shrugged. "I never investigated them."

She hadn't, but I could. Because ... these events. They had to be connected. And, if it was true that Karl's and Peter's ghosts were still around, then there was a high probability that Doug was around too. I could free all of them, and give Sean the closure he needed for that blasted night.

I picked up my phone from my tote and snapped pictures of both articles, plus the article about Sean, Lizzie, and Doug.

I closed the binder and handed it back to Khalisa. "Thank you."

"Don't thank me yet, my child." She took the binder, stood, and returned to the front of her shop. "Say hello to your handsome man."

I frowned at her. "What? You know Sean?"

She nodded. "He came here a few days ago."

What? "Why?"

"I'm afraid you'll have to ask him that," she said, dismissing me. I stared at her a little longer, suddenly wary. I had told Sean about Khalisa and her shop and how the fake bone necklace had helped that night, but I had never thought he would come to her ... and for what?

I made a mental note to investigate that later since now I had something more pressing to worry about. After thanking Khalisa again, I exited the Midnight Cauldron, intent on going to Hotel Monteleone and the Saenger Theater to look for the ghosts of Karl and Peter. Eagerness welled in me, and I finally felt a sliver of hope. When I promised Sean I would try to help Doug, I was wary because I had no idea how. Now, I had a starting point. And, hopefully, it would be a good one.

Because I didn't want to consider the other option I had—to interrogate the dark witch who had been at the haunted house that night. The Lightgrove coven had locked her in the dungeons under the Light Castle. She had been there when Lizzie and Doug were killed too. She was the one who had all the answers. But I wasn't sure if I would be allowed to go near her, or if I even wanted to since she was beyond evil, but the thought had crossed my mind.

As I rounded the corner of Bourbon Street, I bumped into Andrea. Brittany was right beside her.

"Hey, you!" Andrea said, holding my shoulders and steadying me.

"Hi, guys," I said, smiling. Although I didn't have any close friends, I kind of thought these two girls could turn out to be it. "What are you two doing here?"

Brittany showed me the box of beignets in her arms. "We came to buy these."

My mouth watered. "Nice."

"What are you doing here?" Andrea asked.

"Hm ..." I tried thinking of something. Anything. "I came to research something for a class project."

"Oh, cool. What is it about?" Brittany asked.

The memory of Rodd finding me in the castle's library with a stupid book in my hand came to mind. I was in the same pathetic situation here.

"Well ..." I looked around, trying to find a topic that would make sense. My eyes found an apothecary, which promised their potions were brewed by real witches. "It's for my history class," I lied. "We need to write about the Salem trials, and I wanted to talk to real witches." I pointed toward the apothecary, making sure I had a can-you-believe-that face.

The sisters exchanged a look and then smiled big.

"Oh, we want to go too!" Andrea said.

"We love witches and werewolves and ghosts," Brittany said. "Any supernatural stuff, really."

I swallowed hard. "I already talked to them, actually." My voice hitched, and I hoped they didn't catch my lies. Damn it. Here were the two girls I thought I could be friends with, and I was already lying to them. Not good. So not good.

Andrea's smiled faded. "Oh."

"Well." Brittany hooked her arm on mine. "Then that means you can come with us and eat these delicious beignets while we watch horror movies."

I opened my mouth to come up with another excuse but couldn't think of any. Besides, hadn't I already lied enough for one day? Eating beignets and watching horror movies sounded good, but ... what about Doug?

Nothing was stopping me from coming back later, after I spent a couple of hours with the girls. Maybe, if everything worked out, I would even be able to squeeze in an hour or two with Sean before it was time to head back to the castle.

I smiled at them. "All right. Let's go."

12

That night, I couldn't sleep. Since I couldn't stay up at the library without causing trouble with all the business about the runes, I ended up hauling a bunch of books from the library to my bedroom. Because the books were huge and heavy, I made four trips, carrying all that I could.

I was determined to prove to Moira I could do this. Even if I had to practice alone in my bedroom, trying to find my affinity, I would.

On my last trip from the library to my bedroom, I walked by Grace, one of the council members, talking to two younger witches. Her green snake was coiled around her arm. I didn't see many of the council members, or Queen Denise, roaming the Light Castle, so this was unexpected. I nodded as I passed them, not sure how I should address higher-ranked witches when meeting them outside events or gatherings.

I headed down the hallway, in the direction of the stairs, when I heard, "Hazel!"

I turned around and my eyes went wide. "Grace," I muttered as the council member walked toward me. I instantly straightened. "Did you call me, ma'am?"

Ma'am? Seriously?

"Call me Grace, Hazel," she said with a smile. "We're all friends here." Faint wrinkles formed around her eyes, and her graying hair was pulled back into a tight braid. I couldn't tell if she was younger than she looked or older. Like the other council members, she radiated power and elegance, giving me the impression that she was over a hundred years old. Which wasn't that uncommon for powerful witches.

I shifted the heavy books in my arms and eyed the snake. Sometimes it looked like a fake rubber one, but then it showed its tongue, reminding us that it was alive and probably venomous. "Can I do anything for you?"

"I just wanted to check on you." She reached for the books and took half from me.

"You don't need to do that."

"I want to. I'll help you take these to your bedroom." She raised an eyebrow at me. "You are going to your bedroom, aren't you?"

"Yes, ma'am." If I had a free hand to slap my mouth, I would have. "Sorry. It's a habit."

"It's okay. It's refreshing to see younger witches who still think respect is necessary." She took the lead, and we walked toward the stairs. "But I mean it. I'm just Grace."

I smiled. "All right."

We went up the stairs, and I felt like squirming in my

own skin. Why was she walking beside me? Helping with my books?

Finally, at the top of the stairs, she glanced at me. "I just wanted to say I'm impressed with you."

"W-what?" I almost tripped on my own feet. "I ... I thought the council was upset with me. Moira told me I was given two weeks to find my affinity or I'll have to leave."

Grace nodded. "That's true. It was the council decision, but I can honestly say we're all cheering for you. But just because we believe in you and want you to succeed doesn't mean we can disregard our rules. Only witches who prove themselves can stay in the program and become full members. We can't make an exception for you."

I let out a long sigh. "I understand."

"But I see you're trying." She gestured to the books in her arms. "You're working hard and studying and catching up. You at least get an A for effort."

"Shame effort isn't enough."

"I agree, but we're one of the best covens in the world. We have to maintain our standards. I hope you understand that."

"I do." It was the truth. If I was in her place, I would probably have cut me from the program already.

"Like I said, we believe in you." She showed me a warm smile. "I believe in you."

I stared at her, a little shocked that she would even remember who I was. Well, she would, since everyone at the castle was talking about what a disappointment I was.

The fact that she was taking a few minutes of her time to tell me this meant a lot.

"Thank you," I said.

Soon, we were in front of my bedroom door. I opened it and put my books inside, on a small table, then came back to grab the books Grace was carrying.

She handed them to me, the snake in her arm just a couple of inches from my own hand. "Anything I can do for you?"

I opened my mouth to tell her no, when two things came to mind. The lightning and the runes, but I was sure she wouldn't tell me about those, and also the Brotherhood of Purity—they had showed up at one of the campus's dorms a few weeks ago, and a couple of days ago, I saw Rodd and other Light Order soldiers coming back from a tussle with them.

"Is there something going on with the Brotherhood of Purity?" I told her about the occurrences. "It seems they are up to something."

Grace let out a low laugh. "They are always up to something, but you shouldn't worry about it. Focus on your studies and finding your affinity. That's all you should do for now."

I nodded. "Thank you," I said. "For helping with the books, for walking with me, and ... for believing in me."

She reached out and placed a hand on my arm. "Good luck, Hazel."

Then, she turned and walked away, and I stared after her, still a little shocked Grace, a council member, had taken the time to tell me she didn't want me to fail. That gave me more strength and purpose. Somehow, I would prove Moira wrong, and I would become a full Lightgrove witch. Even if I had to abdicate sleep for the next five months.

And that would start now. With a heavy exhale, I closed my bedroom door and went to the pile of books. It would be one long night.

13

THAT NIGHT, I COULDN'T SLEEP. SINCE I COULDN'T STAY UP at the library without causing trouble with all the business about the runes, I ended up hauling a bunch of books from the library to my bedroom. Because the books were huge and heavy, I made four trips, carrying all that I could.

I was determined to prove to Moira I could do this. Even if I had to practice alone in my bedroom, trying to find my affinity, I would.

On my last trip from the library to my bedroom, I walked by Grace, one of the council members, talking to two younger witches. Her green snake was coiled around her arm. I didn't see many of the council members, or Queen Denise, roaming the Light Castle, so this was unexpected. I nodded as I passed them, not sure how I should address higher-ranked witches when meeting them outside events or gatherings.

I headed down the hallway in the direction of the stairs, when I heard, "Hazel!"

I turned around and my eyes went wide. "Grace," I muttered as the council member walked toward me. I instantly straightened. "Did you call me, ma'am?"

Ma'am? Seriously?

"Call me Grace, Hazel," she said with a smile. "We're all friends here." Faint wrinkles formed around her eyes, and her graying hair was pulled back into a tight braid. I couldn't tell if she was younger than she looked or older. Like the other council members, she radiated power and elegance, giving me the impression that she was over a hundred years old. Which wasn't that uncommon for powerful witches.

I shifted the heavy books in my arms and eyed the snake. Sometimes it looked like a fake rubber one, but then it showed its tongue, reminding us that it was alive and probably venomous. "Can I do anything for you?"

"I just wanted to check on you." She reached for the books and took half from me.

"You don't need to do that."

"I want to. I'll help you take these to your bedroom." She raised an eyebrow at me. "You are going to your bedroom, aren't you?"

"Yes, ma'am." If I had a free hand to slap my mouth, I would have. "Sorry. It's a habit."

"It's okay. It's refreshing to see younger witches who still think respect is necessary." She took the lead, and we walked toward the stairs. "But I mean it. I'm just Grace."

I smiled. "All right."

We went up the stairs, and I felt like squirming in my

own skin. Why was she walking beside me? Helping with my books?

Finally, at the top of the stairs, she glanced at me. "I just wanted to say I'm impressed with you."

"W-what?" I almost tripped on my own feet. "I ... I thought the council was upset with me. Moira told me I was given two weeks to find my affinity or I'll have to leave."

Grace nodded. "That's true. It was the council decision, but I can honestly say we're all cheering for you. But just because we believe in you and want you to succeed doesn't mean we can disregard our rules. Only witches who prove themselves can stay in the program and become full members. We can't make an exception for you."

I let out a long sigh. "I understand."

"But I see you're trying." She gestured to the books in her arms. "You're working hard and studying and catching up. You at least get an A for effort."

"Shame effort isn't enough."

"I agree, but we're one of the best covens in the world. We have to maintain our standards. I hope you understand that."

"I do." It was the truth. If I was in her place, I would probably have cut me from the program already.

"Like I said, we believe in you." She showed me a warm smile. "I believe in you."

I stared at her, a little shocked that she would even remember who I was. Well, she would, since everyone at the castle was talking about what a disappointment I was.

The fact that she was taking a few minutes of her time to tell me this meant a lot.

"Thank you," I said.

Soon, we were in front of my bedroom door. I opened it and put my books inside on a small table, then came back to grab the books Grace was carrying.

She handed them to me, the snake in her arm just a couple of inches from my own hand. "Anything I can do for you?"

I opened my mouth to tell her no, when two things came to mind. The lightning and the runes, but I was sure she wouldn't tell me about those, and also the Brotherhood of Purity—they had showed up at one of the campus's dorms a few weeks ago, and a couple of days ago, I saw Rodd and other Light Order soldiers coming back from a tussle with them.

"Is there something going on with the Brotherhood of Purity?" I told her about the occurrences. "It seems they are up to something."

Grace let out a low laugh. "They are always up to something, but you shouldn't worry about it. Focus on your studies and finding your affinity. That's all you should do for now."

I nodded. "Thank you," I said. "For helping with the books, for walking with me, and ... for believing in me."

She reached out and placed a hand on my arm. "Good luck, Hazel."

Then, she turned and walked away, and I stared after her, still a little shocked Grace, a council member, had taken the time to tell me she didn't want me to fail. That gave me more strength and purpose. Somehow, I would prove Moira wrong, and I would become a full Lightgrove witch. Even if I had to abdicate sleep for the next five months.

And that would start now. With a heavy exhale, I closed my bedroom door and went to the pile of books. It would be one long night.

14

I WAS THE FIRST TO ARRIVE AT THE LOUNGE ROOM THE NEXT morning. Moira was second, and she raised an eyebrow at me when she entered the room. Soon, the other girls arrived and we discussed the activities of the past few days —not touching the dark lightning subject, of course—and what we would be doing today.

To Moira's surprise—and mine—I didn't go to class. I stayed at the castle and worked with the other girls all day. I felt guilty for missing classes, but I had to show her I wanted this. I wanted to become a full member of the Lightgrove coven, and I was willing to work hard for it.

But how hard?

At lunch break, I went to the mess hall with the girls and we all had lunch together. As usual, Laini was conceited, acting as if the world revolved around her. The others seemed concerned with what Laini thought of them. However, I ate quickly and left for the garden where Moira and I had practiced. I remembered most of Moira's list, so I followed it from memory and worked through the exercises she had put me through, hoping that maybe, just maybe, something was off that day and that was why I hadn't found my affinity.

After our practice together in the afternoon, the girls and I had dinner in the mess hall and then were dismissed for the day to do whatever. Most girls stayed in the hall and some headed to each other's bedrooms to talk. And I went back to the garden.

I talked to Sean on the phone at least once a day. For some reason, I didn't tell him about the ultimatum the council had given me, but I told him I had to work hard this week. He said he understood, though by the dejected tone of his voice, I kind of doubted he did.

When I thought too hard about Sean and me, I saw no future for us and that made my heart ache. We were too different and I was a witch, a busy witch who needed to work harder than the others to succeed. And he was a human. Would he accept this way of life?

Damn it. Here I was, thinking about that again. It was too soon. Our relationship was too new to think about these things. We had to go day by day and see if it survived this phase. If it did—and I would fight for its survival with everything I had—then I would worry about the future.

That was my routine for the rest of the week, though I did go back to classes on Thursday and Friday, afraid that if I missed too much, I would miss an important quiz or assignment and would fail my classes. However, my excursions out of the castle were quick. I went to class and came back—no meeting with Sean, or Andrea and Brittany, and

I certainly didn't stop by my dorm to get more clothes or books.

Friday night, the girls were chattier than normal during dinner. I could see they all had gotten close during these past two weeks, and it seemed they were finally getting used to me.

"That black fire show hasn't happened again," Cleo said in a low voice. From what I heard, each of us called the event a different name—black fire, lightning, dark flames …

"It's odd how we've been waiting for a next time, right?" Belinda said, seated beside Cleo. "Because it's bound to happen, don't you think?"

From across the table, Laini shrugged. "I don't know. I never saw anything like that, and when I asked my mother about it, she didn't know anything either."

"I asked my mother too," Mei said. She was seated beside Laini. "And my older sister. They have no idea what that was."

"But if you ask me …" Cleo flickered her gaze side to side, making sure nobody was nearby. "I think the council knows exactly what the lightning show was."

"I agree," Laini said. "Unfortunately, I don't think they plan on sharing with us."

"Have you asked your aunt about it, Laini?" I asked.

She turned her eyes to me. "No. I thought about it, but my mother warned me not to bother Aunt Clara. She said that if it was important, Aunt Clara would have told us."

I stared at her. I'd known her mother was a high-ranked witch who was in line to be on the council, but I had no idea her aunt was one of the council members. Maybe I should spend more time with the girls. This way, I could learn more about this kind of stuff.

Although I believed Laini didn't ask her aunt about it, I wasn't convinced the council members didn't know what the lightning and the runes meant.

Later that night, when I was alone in my bedroom, I called my mother. She might be a weak witch, but she was resourceful, and I had to check everywhere I could.

"No, sweetie, I have no idea what that was, and I'm sure none of the books or grimoires I own have anything on that. Why are you asking?"

"It happened again and the council still refuses to talk about it," I explained, pacing in front of my bed. "Actually, they say they don't know what it is or what it means, and since it hasn't hurt anyone, we should forget about it. But, Mom, since when do fire—a black one at that—and runes appear out of nowhere and mean nothing?"

"True, but if the council doesn't know, it's not likely that anyone else will know either."

"That's the thing, I think the council is lying."

She gasped. "Hazel, no. The council would never lie. If they say it's not important, then it isn't."

I sighed. I had momentarily forgotten my mother's crazy obsession with the Lightgrove coven. Of course she would believe every single word they uttered.

"You're right," I said. It wasn't a lie, per se, because I *thought* she was right. I couldn't be sure of it. I forced a loud yawn. "I should go to bed."

"Busy day tomorrow?" Her tone was eager, as if the

idea of being cooped up with other witches all day was exciting.

"Yup. And busy day today too, so I'm tired."

"Then go rest, sweetie. Good night."

"Good night, Mom."

Because of our lineage, I was sure my mother wouldn't have any news for me, but as I ended the call, I realized I did have hope she would surprise me. And, of course, she didn't.

After a quick shower—during which I thought a lot about the runes, but everything that I thought of was a dead end—I put on my pajamas and lay in bed surrounded by thick leather books, and with my phone in my hand.

I called Sean, but he didn't answer, so I sent him a quick text.

Me: *I miss you. Sweet dreams.*

I waited for a few minutes, hoping he would answer, but tiredness won and soon I was snoozing soundly.

15

To my surprise, Moira invited me to go out with her on Saturday evening. I had plans to spend my night with Sean—which he didn't know yet and now never would—but I held my tongue and my curses. I knew, I *knew* she was doing this on purpose. Taking every free moment of my life, making me busy, so busy that I couldn't even catch my breath, so I would tire faster and give up on the program.

Or be kicked out.

Something wasn't right, and it wasn't only with Moira and my training. That morning, I'd woken up and found a reply from Sean on my phone—timed at two in the morning.

Good night was all it said. And for some reason, that didn't sit well with me. I felt like I was losing him, and there was nothing I could do to hold on to him.

The day was busy, though, and I barely had time to think about Sean and our doomed relationship.

In the evening, Moira took me to the French Quarter, of all places, and we walked the streets in silence. My tension and anticipation were on high alert, expecting her to throw something at me out of nowhere. A mission, a question, some magic. Anything.

Surprising me a second time in less than an hour, Moira entered a nondescript door jammed between two shops. She beckoned for me to follow her in. Wary, I stepped inside the small space. The door closed behind us, encasing us in darkness.

"What the ...?" I muttered.

"Wait," Moira said. After a few seconds, my eyes adjusted to the darkness and the shape of a staircase appeared in front of us. "Come," Moira said, starting the climb up the stairs.

"Aren't you going to tell me where you're taking me?" I finally asked.

"We're almost there," was all I got from her.

Illuminated only by a dim light coming from somewhere in the building, we went up three flights of stairs. Then, we stopped in front of a wooden door.

I glanced at Moira. "What is this place?"

She finally looked at me. "Be friendly and respectful. Even if you're not officially a Lightgrove witch, you're under our care."

I raised my eyebrows at her. She called the way she treated me care? Wow, that was quite shocking.

Moira opened the door, revealing a large seating room with plenty of thick rugs and velvet loveseats. The walls had tapestries and landscape paintings. And right in the center of the room stood an older woman and a man.

"Moira," the woman said with a smile. She had long brown hair cascading behind her back, and dark brown eyes. "It's good to see you."

Moira's entire mien changed as she smiled—truly smiled. "You too." She walked to the woman and the two of them embraced. "Thank you for coming."

"Not a problem." The woman leaned closer and said in a lower voice, "I've got to admit I'm curious about what you told me." Then the woman gestured to the man beside her. "You remember my son."

"Of course." Moira shook the man's hand. "I hope the trip here was uneventful."

"It was," the man answered, his voice deep. Like his mother, he had dark brown hair and eyes. There was no denying they were related.

"Sorry for bringing him with me," the woman teased. "He didn't want me to come to a city full of unruly supernaturals by myself."

"It's okay," Moira assured her.

Then the woman's eyes found me standing a few feet behind them. "This is the witch?"

"Yes." Moira beckoned me to approach them. Dutiful, I walked until I was standing by her side. "Hazel, this is Almae. She's originally a Silverblood witch, but she founded a sanctuary for several supernaturals called Unity. And this is her son, Keeran, the Warlock Lord."

I stared at both of them, a little shocked. I had never met another type of witch, much less a warlock! Males of our kind carried the magic gene, but they couldn't access it. But it wasn't true for other kinds of witches.

Moira nudged me hard on the ribs.

"H-hi," I stumbled. "It's a pleasure to meet you." Question was, why the hell was I meeting them?

Almae turned fully to me, her dark eyes full of wonder. "Light witches usually present with an affinity by their sixteenth birthday, but I'm told you're almost nineteen and have no gift. That's quite interesting."

My shoulders sagged, and all I wanted was to bury myself in a hole. Moira called a Silverblood witch here and told her about me? What the hell?

"It's true," I said in a dejected tone.

Almae extended her hand to me. "May I?"

I glanced at Moira, who gave me a sharp nod. Wary, I slipped my hand in Almae's. She held on to me with a tight grip and closed her eyes. I felt her magic, bold and strong, brushing against me, enveloping me like a warm embrace. Almae's brows knitted as she did whatever was she was doing.

I looked at Moira and Keeran, but they didn't seem worried or in a hurry. I shifted my weight, uncomfortable with this.

Finally, Almae let out a long sigh, opened her eyes, and let go of my hand.

"So?" Moira asked. "What did you see?"

See? What was Almae's gift?

The knot in Almae's brows didn't ease as she said, "Nothing."

Moira's eyes bugged. "Nothing? Is that possible?"

"I felt a strong magic wrapped around her. Not just around her magic, which is still buried inside her. It's wrapped around her affinity too, keeping it hidden from us." She glanced at me, as if it was my fault. "This magic is tied around her entire self. I couldn't see anything about her future because of it."

Moira huffed. "I really thought this would work."

"It usually does," Almae said.

Moira shifted her gaze to me. "Could you sense what kind of magic is wrapped around her?"

Almae shook her head. "I couldn't."

"So, if we can't sense it, there's no way of breaking it."

They were all looking at me, but speaking as if I wasn't there. I wanted to scream at them, but for some reason, I couldn't act like that in front of two strangers—two powerful strangers.

"Exactly." Almae reached to me and patted my arm. "I'm sorry, my child, that I couldn't help you more."

"It's okay," I said, still confused about all that had happened in the last few minutes.

Moira inhaled deeply and faced Almae. "Thanks for trying."

"My pleasure," Almae said.

"Tell me, how is the idea of the school for supernaturals going?" Moira asked.

School for what?

A smile spread over Almae's lips. "I'm working on it. I've been meeting with Headmaster Rey of the Blackthorn Hunters Academy and with Queen Thea, who is getting a school for witches ready, to get an idea of all I need. It's more work than I anticipated, but I'm enjoying it." She nodded her head at her son. "Keeran here has been helping me."

He shrugged. "If we're putting supernaturals under one roof, we need to be careful."

"True." Moira nodded. "Tell me something, I heard now that you're out of hiding, you're looking for your sister again. Have you found her?"

Almae's face fell. "I didn't find her, but I learned what happened. She and her lover were killed, I don't know by whom. I also heard she had a daughter and she was around ten or eleven years old when that happened. No one seems to know her name or what happened to her, so now I'm looking for my niece."

"I wouldn't have a clue where to start looking for your niece either, but I'll keep my ears peeled. If I hear something, I'll let you know," Moira said, sounding nice. Ew. "Anyway, thank you so much for coming, Almae. And I'm sorry I've wasted your time."

"Don't worry, Moira." Almae took her hand and shook it. "It was interesting." She glanced at me and winked. "Good luck to you, Hazel."

"Thank you," I said, still feeling out of place.

After another round of goodbyes and good lucks, Moira steered me out of the sitting room and onto the streets of the French Quarter.

But as we left, I couldn't shake the feeling that there was more going on here, and I couldn't figure out what.

16

WE HEADED BACK TOWARD THE ANTIQUE STORE, MOIRA
walking briskly by my side.

"What was that all about?"

Moira huffed. For a moment, I thought she wouldn't
say anything. "Almae has visions of the future, most of the
time. I asked her to come and see your future. I thought
she might catch a glimpse of you using your affinity in the
future. Or find out whatever the hell you'll be doing in the
future." She gave me a side glance. "Like maybe giving up
magic and living as a human."

I frowned at her and purposely chose to ignore her
words. "But she couldn't see anything."

"Exactly." Moira shook her head. "Waste of time."

I opened my mouth, ready to say I was sorry for being
such a disappointment, but I wouldn't give her that satisfaction. "She said something about a magic wrapped
around me, but she doesn't know what it is. Is there a way
we can find out?"

"I don't know," Moira said, her voice tight, tighter than usual. "I'll have to research more about that."

"Careful," I teased. "I'll start to think you care."

Moira glared at me. "I care about the Lightgrove coven and right now, you're one of my initiates. It's my job to care."

I stared at her. That was quite surprising. If someone had asked me, I would have said Moira didn't care at all. But more than that, what the hell was happening here? I couldn't find my affinity, a strange magic was tied around me, and apparently, I didn't have a future.

Or at least one that Almae could see.

A pang of jealousy sliced through my heart as I watched the crowd gathered in the streets of the French Quarter. Every day was big here, but Saturday nights were even more special. Jazz bands played along the sidewalks, performers slipped between the tourists like magicians, and groups wore costumes as if it were Halloween. It was bright and pretty and joyful and contagious.

I smiled, wishing I could have the best of both worlds, but deep down, I knew I couldn't. Besides all this affinity craziness, in five months I would have to choose, and that knowledge made me anxious. If I got to that point. But if I had to choose now, I wouldn't have a pick. Would five months down on this road make a difference? Would I have learned something, done something, become some-thing that would make my choice easier?

Still pondering the different paths in my life, I looked through the outer glass wall of a pub and stopped dead in my tracks.

"What is it?" Moira asked, glancing back.

Sean was inside the pub, sitting alone at the bar, a bottle of beer in one of his hands and an unlit cigarette in the other. His eyes were downcast, and he looked deep in thought. A sudden urge to go in and hug him assaulted me, but I remained frozen in place.

What was he doing here? Why was he here alone?

But I knew the answers to those questions. Sean didn't have any friends, not real friends anyway. It was only me, and I was too busy to spend any time with him. So, instead of moping around alone in his apartment, he decided to go out. I should be happy for him, that he was trying to recover and move on, but that was not what I felt. Guilt mixed with jealousy and disappointment inside my chest.

"I see college isn't the only reason you're so attached to the human world," Moira said, looking at Sean.

I shot her a glare. "This is none of your business."

"Of course it is!" she hissed, keeping her voice low so the people walking past us couldn't make out her words. "It's disrupting your progress, so it is my business. It is the Lightgrove coven's business."

"You—" I shut my mouth before I yelled at her, though I wasn't sure what to say. I would probably say any shit that came to mind just to vent my frustration, and then I would be in even bigger trouble than I already was.

"I know you don't want to hear this, but relationships with humans are difficult," she said. I fought the urge to punch her. "They don't understand our customs, our way of life. They aren't willing to make the same sacrifices we are."

"Some Light Order members are humans."

"Only a handful among hundreds, and those are the rare exception. Most Light Order members are sons of witches. They were raised in our world, with our rules, and our magic. They understand their duty. Most importantly, they understand ours."

Duty.

What was my duty?

My heart was divided in two, and I didn't know how to mend it. Was there a way to mend it? I wasn't so sure anymore.

"Come on." Moira took my elbow and pulled me forward. "We need to go back to the castle."

17

I was supposed to stay at the castle Sunday evening, but I couldn't. I had barely slept Saturday night thinking about Sean—my chest hurt each time the memory of seeing him alone at that bar popped in my mind. And I had been miserable the rest of the day. I had no idea how I focused during the meetings with Moira. Sheer stubbornness, perhaps?

Regardless, I had to talk to Sean. I had to see him, hear his voice, and if he allowed me, embrace him and kiss him and ...

After dinner, I told the girls I had a headache, and then I sneaked out of the castle. Sneaked wasn't the right word, since a few Light Order soldiers saw me leaving the castle and going through the portal—there was no way around them, unfortunately.

Once more, the lights on the windows of his apartment were out, but I rang the intercom anyway. After a couple of minutes, I called his cell phone. I didn't think Sean was sleeping—it was too early—but what if he was? I would wake him up. I had to wake him up.

I called three times and ended up leaving a message for him.

"Sean, we need to talk. I'm at your building, waiting for you. Call me when you can."

Then, I sat down on the steps in front of his building and waited.

Almost thirty minutes later and two bitten-off nails, I saw Sean as he turned a nearby corner, running. After a few seconds, he saw me and slowed his steps until he halted a good ten feet from me.

I stood. "Hi."

Dripping with sweat, he took a long breath before answering, "Hey."

"I called you but ..."

"I left my phone in my room," he said, still catching his breath.

"Have a good run?" I asked, feeling like the lamest girl alive.

"It helps me think."

"About?"

He crossed his arms. "How is witch school?" His tone was sharp, hurt.

I winced. "It's ... much busier and demanding than I thought it would be."

"I noticed."

I took a step toward him and stopped. He didn't seem to want me any closer to him. "Sean, I'm so sorry ... I want to spend more time with you. I want to spend all my time with you, but they are threatening to kick me out. I have to put on a good show for now."

"For the next five months." It was more like four and a half now, but who was counting?

I sighed. "I don't know how long. Maybe less if I can impress my mentor enough."

"And how is that going?"

"Not good."

"And after these five months, Hazel? Won't you have to choose between being with the coven or in this world? Won't you have to quit college?"

"I don't know yet," I said, feeling my frustration escalating. "Maybe I can convince the council to let me finish."

"What if you can't?"

"I don't know!" I shouted. "I don't know," I tried again in my normal tone. "I can't make decisions about something that might or might not happen in five months." Despite trying to hold still, I took another step toward him. "Can't we just take it slow? In a day-by-day way?"

"I am taking it day-by-day, Hazel, and you're never in my days." I flinched at his words. "I didn't see you a single moment this past week."

"I know," I whispered, feeling the tears coming up. I pushed them back. "I'm trying to do the best I can. It'll get better."

"I don't think it will. Even if we can go through the next five months, barely seeing each other, don't you think being a full member of the coven will actually take even more of your time? You'll have new responsibilities and schedules and things to attend to?"

"I haven't decided if I'll stay in the coven after the initiate program."

"The fact that you're so afraid of being kicked out of the program tells me exactly what your choice will be."

I gasped. He ... shit, he was right. Why else would I be working so hard to stay in the program and impress Moira? So she would write a kick-ass report and I would join the Lightgrove coven. But that didn't need to be the end of us.

"There are no rules saying a witch can't be with a human," I explained.

Sean stared at me for a heartbeat. Two. Three. Four. "Maybe I have a rule saying I can't be with a witch."

The air was knocked from my lungs. "You don't mean that." Tearing his eyes from me, Sean walked past me, to the front door of his building. "I don't know what else to say. I don't know what you want me to say."

He paused at the door and glanced at me over his shoulder. "There's nothing else to say. Good bye, Hazel. Good luck with the coven."

And just like that Sean stepped into the building and closed the door behind him.

18

Numb, I walked back to campus. I probably should've headed back to the castle, but I just ... I wasn't thinking, I wasn't feeling. Everything was numb and cold.

I didn't care about the earful I would get from Moira tomorrow morning at check-in. If I went back for check-in. I had classes here later, so what was the point in going all the way there to come back after?

Oh, my head hurt. I couldn't think straight. Nothing made sense anymore.

I halted in front of my building and stared at it. I didn't want to go in. I didn't want to risk facing Krissa or Andrea and Brittany and having them notice my glum mien. They would make me explain what happened and I ... I just didn't know. What had happened?

A meow caught my attention, and I instinctively knew who that was.

Glancing to my right side, I saw the cat seated on a wooden bench as if he was simply waiting for someone.

Me?

"What do you want?" I snapped. "I'm tired of you following me around. Go find someone else to bother."

The cat tilted his head and licked his paw. *This lady is crazy*, he was probably thinking.

And maybe the cat was right.

With a sigh, I sat down on the bench with the cat. I noticed for the first time that he didn't have a collar. A stray cat with such shiny fur? Not likely.

"Are you lost, kitty?" I asked, reaching for him, but retreated my hand before touching him. "Your owner must be worried."

If he had an owner who cared.

Everyone had someone who cared about them, right? I had my mother and Amanda. That was enough.

Tears sprang to my eyes and I felt silly. I wiped at them furiously. What was wrong with me? I wasn't a weak girly-girl. I had never cried for a guy before and wouldn't start now.

Closing my eyes, I took a deep breath. I needed something. I needed to do something to occupy my mind. I needed to get busy right now, otherwise I would cry. I glanced up at the building to where Andrea and Brittany's room was located and saw their lights on. I could invite them to watch a horror movie with me. Ghosts and curses and psycho serial killers were sure to take Sean out of my mind.

Ghosts.

I jumped to my feet, knowing exactly what I could do to occupy my mind.

"Bye, kitty," I whispered as I messed with my phone, calling an Uber.

The Uber arrived less than five minutes later and drove me to Hotel Monteleone. It dropped me across the street from the hotel. I watched the building with a certain feeling of purpose.

My plan was to go around to the hotel's alley and find a way inside—even if I had to use magic to trick an employee or two. The article mentioned Karl had died in the hallway of the third floor, but I thought I could reach him from outside.

I walked normally, as if I intended to enter, but with a glance over my shoulder to make sure no one was paying attention to me, I slipped into the narrow alley leading to the back of the hotel.

Damn, I could sense quite a few ghosts in here. Hadn't I dispatched them all during the last Friday the Thirteenth? Was a dark witch up to something again?

Okay, okay, one thing at a time. I was here to find Karl, so he could lead me to Doug. Sean and I might not be together anymore, but I had promised him I would find Doug, and I never broke my promises.

Hoping no one would come through the side alley, I knelt and drew a circle on the wet, broken concrete floor, then placed the crystals I always carried with me on the north, south, east, and west sides of the circle. I didn't think I needed the crystals to call on ghosts and set them free anymore, but it was a habit, and since my magic could get out of control sometimes, it was better if I did it in the way I was used to.

I closed my eyes and channeled my magic. "*Apparet,*" I said, calling Karl. I sensed him somewhere inside the hotel, fighting against my summon. I channeled more magic into my spell and repeated it, "*Apparet.*"

A faint light appeared in the middle of the circle, and slowly, it morphed into the shape of a young man. He jerked against the bounds of the circle, his ghost-white face looking scared.

"What do you want?" he asked, his voice revealing fear.

"Are you Karl?"

"No," he said too quickly.

"I think you're Karl," I insisted. "I summoned you because I have a couple of questions for you."

"And why should I answer your questions?"

"Because I can set you free." His eyes bugged, and he stopped fighting my magic. "I can send your soul to heaven if that's what you wish. But only after you answer my questions."

"How do I know you're not lying?"

"You'll have to trust me," I said. A moment passed, and he still stared at me with wariness in his pale eyes. "What do you have to lose?"

His shoulders relaxed a tiny bit. "All right. What do you want to know?"

"How did you die?"

"My friend, John, dared me to come here on Halloween night. It was supposed to be haunted, but I thought that was just crap to get tourists interested. Well, it turned out it was true. And then, there was a witch here."

"A dark witch?"

"What do you mean?"

"Was the witch evil?"

"Yeah, I mean, she was calling more ghosts from what looked like a cut in the middle of the air, and she was ordering them around. She saw my friend and me, and they attacked us. My friend was able to get away, but I wasn't."

"What happened after?"

"She sent most of the ghosts away."

I frowned. "What do you mean?"

"She just left, using her magic to command ghosts to follow her."

"Most, but not all. Do you know why?"

Karl shrugged. "Why a witch kills people and takes ghosts? Are you freaking kidding me? I have no idea!"

"Okay, calm down, I'm trying to understand what is going on."

"I don't want to understand. I want to—"

A crystal rolled out from its place and Karl's ghost flickered in and out.

"What the ...?" I muttered.

Half a second later, another crystal was pushed back from its place, and Karl was gone. I looked around, but didn't see anything. I knelt beside the fallen crystals, trying to figure out what could have possibly moved them, when a chill breeze swept through me, bringing more than just cold. I stiffened, intuitively knowing something was wrong.

Then, three figures jumped me. Three males dressed in black pants, shirts, vests, and wearing long red cloaks with hoods that concealed their faces.

"Well, well, well. What do we have here?" one of the Brotherhood of Purity members said.

My blood turned to ice and I stepped back. "What do you want?"

Stupid, stupid question.

"Do we really have to answer that?" another one asked. He walked to the circle and rubbed the tip of his boot on the edge of the circle, erasing my drawing. The circle was undone.

Shit.

Quick, Hazel, think!

"Just take her and let's go," the third one said.

They advanced on me, and I called upon the wind coursing through the alley.

"*Ventus.*" The wind pushed them back and I ran to the street.

But before I could reach the end of the alley, something snaked around my ankles and jerked me back.

I screamed as I fell on the wet, dirty ground and was pulled back by the black leather rope around my ankles. Panic filled my chest and my blood roared in my ears.

"Where do you think you're going, little witch?"

"*Redono,*" I said, ordering the rope to untie, but it didn't work.

"Don't bother," one of the hunters said. "Our weapons are all enchanted against witch magic."

Their weapons, but not them.

I called the wind again. The invisible wall pushed them back, farther than before. I kept muttering spells while I worked to get free from the ropes. "*Ventus.*" Another blast of wind pushed them back. "*Petram.*" Little pebbles from the ground flew at them like bullets from a gun. Finally, the ropes loosened, and I struggled to get them off me.

The hunters groaned and cursed as they dodged the pebbles.

Finally free from the rope, I scurried to my feet and turned to run again. And then more ropes wound around me—my ankles, my waist, and my shoulders. My arms were pinned, and this time, when I hit the ground, there was nothing to soften my fall. I bumped my head hard against the concrete. Pain exploded inside my skull and I felt like I was drowning.

"There's no way you can escape us, little witch," one of the hunters said.

"Take her," another said.

Darkness surrounded me and I tried to fight it. I tried calling on light, I tried calling for help, but my mind was on fire and my voice was gone. There was nothing else I could do.

A meow echoed through the alley as a black cat—the same damned cat?—jumped from one of the windows and landed on top of one of the men. The cat scratched at the Brotherhood members, keeping them busy.

Pushing through the pain in my skull, the numbness in my limbs, the dizziness in my head, I called my magic to untie the ropes. I jerked and jerked, until finally they loosened and I scurried from them and out of the alley.

I almost ran over a couple on the sidewalk, but I didn't

stop running. I only stopped when I saw the line of cabs at the corner of the hotel and jumped into one.

"Take me to Towland," I said, my voice winded.

As the cab sped up, I relaxed in the seat, taking a moment to realize I had been attacked by the Brotherhood and I had narrowly escaped.

19

THE CAB DROPPED ME OFF OUTSIDE THE DORM COMPLEX. Thankfully, it was late and not many people saw as I limped to my building and dragged myself up the stairs to my bedroom.

Every time I heard footsteps or doors opening and closing, I gritted my teeth and hid myself. Hopefully, none of these people were Krissa, or Andrea and Brittany. I didn't care if others saw me, but if the three of them found me, then I would have to lie.

And what would my lie be?

I had no idea what to tell them.

All I could think was that holy shit, the Brotherhood of Purity had almost captured me. If it weren't for that damn cat, I would be gone now. Taken to their place. Or killed.

I shuddered and the pain in my head worsened. I desperately needed some pain medicine and sleep, but I probably shouldn't sleep right now, in case I had a concussion. No, I should take a shower and assess the damage to my body. Make sure nothing else was badly hurt or bleeding.

With a sigh, I unlocked my room's door and stepped in. I didn't turn on the lights in case Krissa was sleeping. I didn't want to wake her up, and I didn't want her to see me like this.

But it was too late.

"There you are," a deep voice rang through the room.

The lamp on my nightstand turned on, giving the room a dim light, and illuminating the Brotherhood member who held Krissa by the throat, a knife pointed to her stomach.

Krissa's eyes were two huge, wild balls, and she trembled from head to toes.

I spread my hands. "Let her go."

"I will when you surrender," the man said.

I gritted my teeth. Damn it. I didn't want to surrender, but I couldn't let him hurt Krissa too.

However, in the two seconds I stared at him, at the knife pressed against Krissa's belly, one new thought came to my mind. When I was attacked in the alley, I had thought it had been a coincidence, that the Brotherhood was hunting witches randomly, or they had been out doing something else and I stumbled in their way.

But now, there was a Brotherhood member inside my room, threatening my roommate in case I didn't surrender.

They were after me.

But why?

Well, I wouldn't give them the satisfaction of taking me. As quickly as I could, I called my magic and flung my hand. Without me uttering a word, the lamp flew from the nightstand, hitting the man in his head. He grunted and put a hand over his injury, letting go of Krissa. She slipped to the floor.

I raced to her, but only gave one step.

An arm wound around my waist and something was pressed in front of my mouth and nose. I yelled, but a piece of cloth muffled my scream. I jerked, fighting with every inch of strength I had, but the arms around me were too strong. I tried not to breathe, but it was hard not to.

In seconds, the world spun into darkness.

And I lost.

CONTINUE READING HAZEL'S ADVENTURES WITH BOOK 2, *The Midnight Flame*!

BONUS: want to read an exclusive scene from Sean's POV? Download it here!

To read a special and exclusive book about another light witch, join my Facebook Group and find the book called *The Light Witch* to download on the "featured" tab!

FLIP THE PAGE TO READ A SHORT STORY ABOUT ARIANNA'S death—the founder of the Lightgrove Witches!

THANK YOU

THANK YOU FOR READING *THE MIDNIGHT SPELL*!

Reviews are very important for authors. If you liked my book, please consider leaving a review on your favorite online retailer and/or on Goodreads and/or Bookbub, please!

DID YOU LIKE THIS BOOK? YOU CAN CHECK OUT OTHER BOOKS of mine:

The Night Calling (Rite World: Night Wolves book 1): she was abandoned by her mate, left in the hands of a terrible half-demon ... but now he's back and ready to claim her.

The Darkest Vampire (Rite World: Vampire Wars book 1): a witch releases a dark vampire from a curse, and becomes inadvertently bonded to him.

The Demon Kiss (Rite World: Blackthorn Hunters Academy book 1): a fast-paced story about a young woman who finds out she's a demon hunter, and the half-demon intent on protecting her against all evil.

The Vampire Heir (Rite World 1: Rite of the Vampire): a dark and mysterious paranormal romance about a vampire and a young woman with a secret.

The Warlock Lord (Rite World 4: Rite of the Warlock): a thrilling and kick-ass paranormal romance about a were-wolf and warlock.

The Wolf Forsaken (Rite World 7: Rite of the Wolf): a heat-wrenching tale about a lost wolf shifter and a fae princess on the run.

Heart Seeker (The Fire Heart Chronicles book 1): an urban fantasy series about a young woman who finds herself at the center of a mysterious supernatural world.

Destiny Gift (The Everlast Series book 1): a post-apocalyptic urban fantasy series about a young woman with a special power that can save the world.

DON'T FORGET TO SIGN UP FOR MY NEWSLETTER TO FIND OUT about new releases, cover reveals, giveaways, and more!

If you want to see exclusive teasers, help me decide on covers, read excerpts, talk about books, etc, join my reader group on Facebook: Juliana's Club!

ABOUT THE AUTHOR

While USA Today Bestselling Author Juliana Haygert dreams of being Wonder Woman, Buffy, or a blood elf shadow priest, she settles for the less exciting—but equally gratifying—life as a wife, a mother, and an author. She resides in North Carolina and spends her days writing about kick-ass heroines and the heroes who drive them crazy.

Subscribe to her mailing list to receive emails of announcement, events, and other fun stuff related to her writing and her books: www.bit.ly/JuHNL

For more information:
www.julianahaygert.com

facebook.com/julianahaygert

twitter.com/julianahaygert

instagram.com/juliana.haygert

goodreads.com/juliana_haygert

pinterest.com/julianahaygert

bookbub.com/authors/juliana-haygert

youtube.com/julianahaygert

tiktok.com/@julianahaygert

ALSO BY JULIANA HAYGERT

To find links and more info, go to:
www.julianahaygert.com/books/

Shorts
Into the Darkest Fire

Standalones
Daughter of Darkness

Rite World: Night Wolves
The Night Calling (Book 1)
The Night Burning (Book 2)
The Night Hunting (Book 3)
The Night Rising (Book 4)

Rite World: Vampire Wars
The Darkest Vampire (Book 1)
The Darkest Witch (Book 2)
The Darkest Magic (Book 3)

Rite World: Lightgrove Witches
The Midnight Test (Book 1)
The Midnight Spell (Book 2)
The Midnight Flame (Book 3)
The Midnight Secret (Book 4)

Rite World: Blackthorn Hunters Academy
The Demon Kiss (Book 1)
The Hunter Secret (Book 2)
The Soul Bond (Book 3)

The Shadow Trials (Book 4)
The Infernal Curse (Book 5)

Rite World
The Vampire Heir (Book 1)
The Witch Queen (Book 2)
The Immortal Vow (Book 3)
The Warlock Lord (Book 4)
The Wolf Consort (Book 5)
The Crystal Rose (Book 6)
The Wolf Forsaken (Book 7)
The Fae Bound (Book 8)
The Blood Pact (Book 9)

The Wyth Courts
Winter King (Book 1)
Spring Warrior (Book 2)
Summer Prince (Book 3)
Autumn Rebel (Book 4)

The Fire Heart Chronicles
Heart Seeker (Book 1)
Flame Caster (Book 2)
Earth Shaker (Book 2.5)
Sorrow Bringer (Book 3)
Soul Wanderer (Book 4)
Fate Summoner (Book 5)
War Maiden (Book 6)

The Everlast Series
Destiny Gift (Book 1)
Soul Oath (Book 2)
Cup of Life (Book 3)
Everlasting Circle (Book 4)

Willow Harbor Series
Hunter's Revenge (Book 3)

Siren's Song (Book 5)

Breaking Series
Breaking Free (Book 1)
Breaking Away (Book 2)
Breaking Through (Book 3)
Breaking Down (Book 4)